Rik Toil had everything a man could want, money, fast cars, women desperate for his attention.

So why did Eric Tolland, the man behind the image feel so bored by it all? After doing whatever was necessary to make his skateboarding company successful, Eric felt lost.

Mimi Ferguson was no one's idea of a sk8er grl but she was a damn good art director.

She may have always been Mimi the meek but it is time for this mouse to roar.

She was his perfect match if only he can convince her of that.

Escape to the Lovers and Other Strangers world today. This contemporary romance series travels across the US with stops in Boston, Las Vegas and the Southwest, Seattle, and Chicago. With each new book you'll find characters that feel like friends and catch up with past favorites lives. .

Also by L.C. Giroux

Fall Into His Arms
More Lovers and Other Strangers Series Books
Pay Back
His Deception
Lovers and Other Strangers Boxed Set:
The Boston Stories
Second Chance at Salvation
All In
Where's My Cowboy?
Lovers and Other Strangers Boxed Set: Salvation New Mexico
Skater's Girl
...And Keep Her
Love Stranger than Fiction
Lovers and Other Strangers Boxed Set:
Seattle
Just Her Type
Plan Brady
This Day Forward

Series Short Stories:
Wild Child
The Day Before the Night Before Christmas
Cupid Must Be Irish

Skater's Girl

Lovers and Other Strangers Book Seven

L.C. Giroux

www.lcgiroux.com

L.C. Giroux
P.O. Box 628482
Middleton, WI 53562-8482
www.justpublishyourself.com

Publisher's Note: This is a work of fiction. Names, characters, places, and incidents are a product of the author's imagination. Locales and public names are sometimes used for atmospheric purposes. Any resemblance to actual people, living or dead, or to businesses, companies, events, institutions, or locales is completely coincidental.

Book Layout ©2013 BookDesignTemplates.com

Ordering Information:
Quantity sales. Special discounts are available on quantity purchases by corporations, associations, and others. For details, contact the "Special Sales Department" at the address above.

Skater's Girl/ L.C. Giroux -- 2nd ed.

Author's Note:

This book has been kicking around in my head for a while. The hero Eric Tolland originally showed up in my second book, <u>Pay Back</u> but he was around well before that. When I first started writing I read <u>Beyond Heaving Bosoms: The Smart Bitches Guide to Romance Novels</u> by Sarah Wendell and Candy Tan to get a broader overview of the field. Sci Fi romance and even paranormal still confound me. If you haven't read the book I highly recommend it. These women are smart, literate, and hysterically funny.

So what does that book have to do with this one? At one point they are discussing hero archetypes and one of them mentions wishing someone would write a romance with a vegetarian skateboarder as that would be the most unlikely kind of romance hero. Well, after two guys in wheelchairs maybe. Yes, Eric is different but I think you'll like him just the same. Mimi on the other hand is as unlikely a heroine in her own way but I think too many women can relate to her.

For any story there are bunches of people that influence how it gets on the page. For this story there were even more. I won't kid you, I knew nothing about skateboarding, other than it looked cool, before I sat down with Austin at Freedom Skate in Madison WI. He was amazingly generous with his time and patience. Eric's character isn't based on him but the height, laid back generosity, and charm could have been.

I also need to thank the girls and guys at Gillware Data Recovery. Yeah, it sounds random but they literally saved this story and everything I'd ever written when my hard drive went to the big tech dump in the sky. They were like the perfect romance hero, kind, patient, took care of business, and got all my data back to me in three days. Okay, that last part may be the start of another unlikely hero. Hmm, the hot IT guy... there might be something there.

L. C. Giroux

Skater's Girl

Chapter One

"Slate!" the director yelled.

A bored out of his mind intern walked to the center of the set. "Rik Toil Boards summer promo spot end clip. Take thirty-one." Eric didn't miss the glance and smirk at him when the guy slammed the clapper down.

"Okay. Action!"

Out of the corner of his eye, he watched the skate team start to drop on to the ramps that would launch them into the air over his head. He didn't even flinch when they looked like they would crash in the air over him. These guys—and girls—could do this stuff in their sleep. Unfortunately, he felt like he was sleepwalking.

"Cut! Eric, dude, we need that 'I'm the great Rik Toil' smile and you to throw your arms out like we practiced, when they get about halfway down the ramps." Eric was about two seconds from going crazy on this asshole. Right now,

Eric Tolland, the man, was hating being Rik Toil, the caricature. Eric balled his fists like he wanted to punch somebody.

"Uh, why don't we take a break," yelled Steve Frey, as usual the voice of reason. The director looked over at Eric's chief financial officer and smirked.

"Hey, it's your money."

"Yeah, it is and you would be wise to remember we can take our money and go hire another director." It always cracked Eric up when his best friend went all corporate bad-ass on someone since he was the most laid-back guy Eric had ever known.

Two hours later, Steve slammed the door to Eric's office.

"You want to tell me what that was all about?"

Eric didn't turn around, though he could have cared less about the view outside the window. He took a deep breath.

"I'm sorry. I should have just canceled the commercial with the shitty mood I've been in."

"Talk to me. Or do I need to resort to blackmail?"

Eric wondered when had he become such a jerk and looked at the only man brave or crazy enough to smile back at him right now.

"Oh, really? Think about the things I know about you—might raise a few eyebrows in financial circles."

Steve just started laughing at him.

"Seriously, when you said you wanted to start putting your art on skateboard decks and could I help you out with the business plan, did you really think it could lead to a multi-million dollar company?" Steve waved his hand around Eric's office. Eric took a good look at the best view of Pike Place Market and the harbor in Seattle. His office was all sleek chrome and glass. The cliché of the successful CEO he had thought he wanted. The walls were hung with pictures of their skate team or some of his best-selling decks with his art on them. Okay, that part meant something to him. He had absolutely no reason to feel like shit but right now all of it left him cold.

"Okay, no, I didn't, but you don't sometimes miss the struggle?"

"You mean worrying about where we were going to get the money to build the next shipment of decks, or driving the boards to the

shops ourselves because we don't have the cash
to pay for a delivery company? No, can't say as I
do. So is all this about being Rik Toil?"

Eric was never sorry he'd ended up with
Steve as a roommate freshman year. At first
glance, they should have hated each other since
Eric was an art guy and Steve was all business
but their personalities meshed and hanging out
together made the other one forget their
troubles. Eric had known then Steve was the guy
to go to when he had his business idea. They
decided it would be easier to market the boards
with the over-the-top Rik Toil character as
opposed to geeky artist Eric Tolland.

"Yeah, part of it; okay, a lot of it. God, I am
really starting to hate that guy."

"Mmm, yeah, I know what you mean. The guy
has more money than he knows what to do with,
gets to hang out backstage with musicians, a
gorgeous penthouse, and hot women hanging off
him every time he goes out. Yeah, it really sucks
to be that guy. Trade you. You be the boring
accountant for a while and I'll be the suave
playboy with all the toys."

"Yeah, don't think so. We've already figured
out I should never do anything with the books."

Steve groaned. "Don't remind me! Why don't you get out of here for a while? Get on your board. Hey, for old time's sake you can drop off the RFP at MDC instead of paying for a courier."

"You do realize you sound like a total geek when you speak in acronyms, right?"

"You do realize I am your best friend, which makes you an even bigger geek, right?"

"Just give me the damn proposal so I can take it to the ad agency." Eric smiled at his best friend and chief financial officer. Okay, so their common geekiness is what really bonded them in college. That, and their shyness around women.

***

I will not cry, I will not cry! was all Mimi could repeat to herself. The elevator was taking forever to get to the lobby. She was huffing and puffing to keep the tears at bay. How dare they! How. Dare. They! The blasted things were her ideas; how dare they use someone else to present them. The elevator doors opened and she dashed out across the lobby; she ran headlong to get outside. She was so angry, she thought she'd be sick if she didn't get some air. She ran to the steps and flung herself down just as a guy flew over her. He missed her by inches. She couldn't contain her sobbing any longer as she watched him crash at her feet.

"Lady, look out..." He stopped when he saw her tears. "I couldn't hope so beautiful a woman would be crying over me." He stood and took her hand, bending over it and he kissed her fingers lightly.

Mimi was shocked, so shocked she stopped crying and started to laugh. *Did this menace of a man just call her beautiful?* "I wasn't crying for... I... I was crying before you got here," she said softly. "Are you alright, though? Nothing's broken, I hope?"

"I'm fine, nothing but a couple of bruises. There is a reason everyone harps at you to wear a helmet. Now who would be villain enough to make a breathtaking woman like you cry, since it wasn't me you were shedding tears for?"

"Oh." Her sob caught in her throat. He was being so nice and he was handsome and had such understanding eyes. His compliments were appreciated after the nightmare of the staff meeting. What would it hurt to tell this stranger about her horrible morning? He was just a skateboarder, probably a messenger; he seemed a little old to be hanging out on the steps of her office building. "I'm an art director at Mitchell, Day, and Comstock, one of the big ad agencies in town. I came up with a bunch of ideas for a skateboard ad campaign. They all thought the ideas were great but I shouldn't be allowed to even sit in on the pitch because I'm...I...They said..."

"You don't look like a skateboarder?" he said.

"That would have been a heck of a lot nicer but yes, that was the idea."

"You know that is illegal, right?"

"It is a lot of things but they are going to get away with it anyway. Who is going to stop them? I can't risk losing my job to fight them. Anyway, it really only is a couple of the guys and they are just pigs." She smiled at the thought of the bunch of them grubbing away at a trough.

"When you smile you go from merely beautiful to absolutely radiant."

She searched his face for some hint he was being smarmy but there was nothing to suggest he was being anything but honestly complimentary. He was more than merely beautiful himself. His sandy hair was long but it went well with the tanned planes of his face. His nose was slightly hawkish but it kept his face from being pretty. His lips were full and sensual. Mimi shivered, wondering what it would feel like to kiss them. She blinked to bring her thoughts back to the real world. His eyes were a mix of blue and green that she had only seen on color cards. When he caught her staring at him, he smiled and faint crinkles spread from his eyes.

She quickly looked at her lap and then glanced back up at him. "Thank you." He reached for her hand and without even thinking she gave it to him. He gently pulled her to her feet but the angle was odd and she ended up falling against him, wrapping her arms around him to steady herself. He wrapped his arms around her also. They stood like that for just a little too long. Mimi was surprised he was so much taller than her. At 5'10", she was not a tiny girl by any measure.

"Thank you, too." He whispered in her ear. "This is the best thing to happen all day." His words startled her back to her senses and she pulled away, leaving him standing there smiling at her. "Are you going to be okay to go back in there now?" he finally asked.

"Yes, I think so. Thank you for the pep talk."

"Wasn't any trouble at all."

Mimi turned and started walking away. She glanced back over her shoulder as the messenger waved to her. What an unusual man!

Eric shook his head. When had he turned into Prince Charming? Watching her walk away, he was struck by the sway of her hips in the tight skirt. She moved like a dancer but with a softer, tempting body. She was breathtaking in a way that had gone out of style in the Renaissance. Her skin was pale and felt like silk. She was all lush curves. Even her dark hair had waves, begging for his fingers to catch. Her full red lips were a perfect cupid's bow set off by rosy cheeks with a dimple, even when she was crying. Her eyes, even through tears, were a stunning hazel with flashes of gold and green.

She couldn't have been more different than the women he was surrounded by. Was that the reason he wanted to see her again? He'd been so taken with her, he hadn't gotten her name. Hey, she was his own personal Cinderella. Just the thought made him smile. He needed coffee before facing the ad guys. Hadn't she said she worked at an ad agency, too? He couldn't remember which one now. She rattled him and he liked it. Was that the problem with his life? Was he bored with how easy everything had become? She would definitely be an antidote to boredom.

When Mimi got back to the office, Gerry was waiting for her. Gerry was the lucky art director chosen to present her ideas and while he was not a bad guy, he was not about to stick his neck out for her, either.

"Mimi, I feel really bad about this. I just don't want to rock the boat, you know?"

"So you have no problem presenting my ideas as your own?"

"I'm not going to do that. I can present the ideas as the art department's, and if we get the account then you can have it. I don't agree with what those son-of-a-bitches said before and if I were higher in the food chain I'd tell them so but..."

"Aw, heard about the little dust-up in the meeting. I volunteered to pitch it for you but they thought a guy would be better. Someone needs to tell the higher-ups sex sells even when you are pitching a campaign," Sharon purred. All of Mimi's instincts said to run but as usual, Sharon hadn't actually done anything truly obnoxious. Mostly she was oddly friendly and never lost a chance to let everyone know just how sexy she was. Mimi could always count on Sharon inviting her out with "just the 'girls" and this was no exception. "So, Meems." She hated that nickname. Her name was two syllables— how hard was it to say? "You're still coming out tonight, right?"

"Um, sure, I guess." Why was she saying yes? The hell with it; she'd go. She'd have one drink and then she'd go home—and think about the skateboarding Prince Charming she met. She would never see him again but that didn't mean she couldn't fantasize about him.

***

"See, this is how us anonymous people live. No hot chicks hanging around waiting for our attention, no VIP lounges, ignored by the wait staff. Does this make you feel better about being Rik Toil?"

"Actually, this feels great!" Eric grinned from ear to ear.

"You are a sick puppy." Steve shook his head at him.

"You bet!" Eric grinned back. He stretched out in the booth and nursed the beer they were finally able to snag from the waitress. His eyes scanned the crowd on the dance floor. Lots of girls trying too hard to get attention. This kind of music wasn't really his thing. If he was just listening then he liked skate punk or reggae but if he was going to make a fool of himself dancing then he wanted to at least be able to touch the woman he was dancing with. He wondered what Cinderella would be like to dance with. Thinking about all her soft skin and soft curves had him gulping some cold beer down to clear his head. Searching for her hadn't worked out like he'd hoped. He could haunt the building she had gone into but that seemed a little over the top, even for him. Of course she had to take lunch or come out again sometime, right?

Eric looked down at his glass and saw both his and Steve's were empty. Getting the waitress' attention again didn't seem likely. Maybe Steve had a point about the attention not sucking.

"Hey, 'nother round?" he said to his buddy.

"I'll buy, you fly?"

"Sure, the joys of being freaky tall: the bartender can actually see me." As a skateboarder, it was weird being so tall. It meant there were tricks he could never do; all the balance points were wrong and too high off the ground. The best riders were short, usually well under six feet. He loved the freedom and being locked in when he was riding but learned pretty early his talents were in other areas. As he walked toward the bar, he saw her. He did a quick U-turn and went back to Steve.

"She's here!"

"Who?"

"The girl, Cinderella, from the steps."

"Cool. Why are you standing here then? Go all Rik Toil on her and whisk her off to your evil lair."

"That is just it. I don't want to be Rik Toil. I want her to like plain old Eric Tolland, geek artist."

"That is a lot tougher sell, dude. What are you gonna do?"

"I don't know. Don't wait around for me, though."

"Oh, I think I may need to stick around and watch, you know, for the entertainment value."

"You know, you really can be an asshole."

"No, I really just have no life. So where is she?" Eric pointed her out and Steve looked at him like he was crazy. "She's..."

"Beautiful? Perfect? Sensual?"

"I was going to go with tall but I suppose those are good, too. So go ahead, Casanova—I'll be taking notes."

Why had she let Sharon talk her into this? Her head was pounding with the crowd noise and the smell of stale beer made her vaguely sick. Being around Sharon always left her feeling like one of the dancing elephants in the old cartoon. It didn't matter how graceful or pretty she told herself she was, as tall and big as she stood she was still the elephant. A bar stool opened up and she jumped on it. At least sitting down she was shorter. Sharon slid up and yelled in her ear they should mingle. No way was she giving up her bar stool and motioned the bartender to give her another cranberry and vodka. She should just leave. The only guys that even talked to her at places like this were usually short guys with something to prove. Not that she had anything against short guys; actually, she sort of felt an odd kinship with some of them but she couldn't help feeling even bigger and more awkward around them.

That was the hardest part of being the big girl. She drew attention when really she would have preferred to just hide in the background. Her sister Audi was the one who liked to be in the spotlight. Which was good since she was the lead singer of a band. Mimi sighed for about the hundredth time since she had gotten there. If Audi were here she could cut loose and have fun; of course every guy in the place would be looking at her sister. Sometimes it was hard to believe they could even be related. Of course the last three guys she had started going out with turned into total fanboys the minute they found out she was related to the Harridan's Rawdy Maudy and then had only hung around long enough to try to hook up with her lead singer sister. Audi never gave them a second look, as big sisters went she was the best.

Sharon walked back to where she was sitting and gave her the evil eye.

"I thought you were going to have some fun?"

"I am having fun, while I sit here and drink my drink."

"You're supposed to be walking around with me."

"Sorry, my feet hurt." Why did she feel she needed an excuse? Mimi suddenly knew she was being watched. This wasn't her usual feeling of someone looking at her and seeing all her flaws. This was primal; she was the prey and they were the predator. Wait, no, she didn't feel afraid exactly—just keyed up, alert. She stuck the straw of her drink in her mouth and peeked over the top of her glass. No one in that direction was paying any attention to her. She was smack up against the bar so it wasn't coming from there either. She turned in a way she hoped looked nonchalant and peered over Sharon's shoulder. Her mouth dropped open and she gasped. Damn, he started grinning, which meant somehow over the noise he'd heard her. Prince Charming, in all his lean animal glory, started walking towards her. That was what the feeling was. She wasn't the prey; he was stalking a mate, at least for tonight. The thought made her go soft and shiver.

"Mimi, are you listening to me? I want to walk around and I want you to come with me!" Sharon was getting angrier by the minute. It was all Mimi could do to swallow at the moment. She couldn't take her eyes off him. In her head, he was just "the Messenger" like he was some kind of super hero. In her daydreams, she had stripped him down and licked up one side of him and down the other. She wouldn't dare in real life but that was what fantasies were for: doing things you wouldn't do in a hundred million years.

He stood there with his thermal shirt pushed to his elbows and his arms crossed. The way the shirt and the pose defined his chest made her mouth water. The long baggy cargo shorts he wore should have hidden most everything from the waist down. But the way they rode low on his hips made her wish she could just yank on them and see what else was there.

This guy was all kinds of wrong for her. She needed a man who wasn't afraid to be in charge but was still self-assured enough to give up control once in a while. She was pretty driven in her career, despite the stuff that went on today, and couldn't really see herself dating a guy her age who was still skateboarding on the building steps. But whoa, was he good to look at. He moved around Sharon like she wasn't even there and stared into her eyes.

"Hey, Cinderella."

"Hey." *Great time to be completely tongue tied!*

"I looked everywhere for you when I finally came to my senses and realized you hadn't given me your name or any way to find you."

"Oh, Mimi." She struggled to fill her lungs since there seemed to be no air left in the room. Why didn't he stop staring at her? "My name is Mimi."

"Hiya tall, blonde, and handsome, my name is Sharon." He looked her over like she was a bug. That made Mimi giggle; that was not the typical reaction Sharon got from men. Hyper-blonde, curvy, legs for miles, and giving off waves of availability usually turned heads her way without her having to even open her mouth. Being dismissed put her in a snit.

"Mimi, let's get out of here. Obviously this place lets in all kinds of losers." Now she was trying to stare down Prince Charming but it came off as laughable since she wasn't even up to his shoulders.

"Mimi, did you want to leave?" he asked. Those teal eyes looked into her and she could only blink back.

"Mimi! You don't even know his name." Sharon was annoying but she did have a point. Mimi returned his gaze and cocked her head as if to say, "Well..."

"Eric Tolland, at your service." He took her hand and gave her a quick kiss on the back of it like he had done that morning. Her breath caught in her chest. "Stay." How could he make the one word sound so seductive?

"It would be easier if you had a friend for her," she whispered in his ear. She felt like she had fallen down the rabbit hole. She was usually the odd man out when it was her and Sharon.

He turned to look at Sharon again and told her, "My buddy has a whole booth to himself over there." He pointed out the booth he was talking about. She could have sworn she heard Sharon purr. "Word of warning, though, he's an accountant." Sharon's purr turned into a snarl.

"No way. I don't do charity work." Mimi's mouth dropped open. What a bitchy thing to say! The guy was cute enough. Sharon stomped off but not before she yelled over her shoulder that Mimi was on her own.

"I thought she would never leave," he said, grinning at her. "Let's get out of here."

"I'm not going anywhere with you." She was attracted to the guy but she wasn't crazy.

"You want to do what I have in mind right here?"

Her eyes went round.

"What do you have in mind?" Okay, she sounded like an idiot now, but his sexy chuckle pinned her to her seat.

"I was thinking..." She bit her lip and he stared at it like he was starving. Then he closed his eyes and licked his lip. Her stomach did a fluttery thing she'd never felt before. "Ah, see, you bite your lip like that, and now all I can think about doing are naughty things."

"Good thing I'm not leaving then." She laughed but his eyes got greener and he moved in closer.

"I could do naughty things to you here."

"Wha...What?"

"I can tell how turned on you are. As wound up as you are right now, I'll bet I could get you off without touching you below say, the shoulders." She looked at him like he was crazy. Hell, he was.

"Here? Now? I'm not taking my clothes off in public! You are insane!"

"Nope, you don't need to take your clothes off...yet. Well, maybe slip your neckline a little to the side so I can get to that creamy skin of yours."

She bit down on her lip again to keep from groaning but then remembered what he had said and she didn't want to add any fuel to the fire. *Wait a minute, this whole thing was absurd.* It wasn't possible, well, at least not for her. She was going to call his bluff and then he'd back off and go hit on Sharon or someone like her.

"I don't believe you." She sat up straighter, and then decided he should really see her. Guys didn't act like she was some delectable little morsel, ever, once they got a good look at her. She stood up and even in her heels he was still a good four inches taller than her. Okay, but they were kitten heels. He leaned in towards her and she could feel the heat from his body. Or maybe it was her body sending out the sauna signals.

"You want to do this standing up, little Miss Mimi?"

Somehow the way he said her name made her feel delicate and cherished. Okay, she was losing it now. She didn't even know this guy. But the part of her that always felt like the dancing elephant blushed and batted her eyes at him.

"I still don't believe you but you can try. You can't touch me below the shoulders and you can't undress me..." She had a flash of inspiration! "Oh, and you can't use your hands!" She crossed her arms to put the "so there" on the end. Except he just laughed.

"You want hardball, you get hardball, miss. Have it your way."

He leaned forward so he was whispering in her ear. "Every time you sigh, I'm going to nibble this spot right here." Then he swirled his tongue lightly at the spot just below and behind her ear. Which naturally made her sigh, so he grazed his teeth over it this time. Which made her whole body quake. He pulled back now.

"Still don't think I can? Do you want to make a bet?"

Hell, at this point she could barely think.

"Sure." She was trying to keep her eyes from crossing.

"If I succeed, then you agree to go out with me on a date of my choosing. I can promise you there will be hands used on that one." She sighed and he leaned forward slowly like he was daring her to flinch and gently bit down on the sensitive spot again. Her knees almost buckled. "I said..."

She nodded her head, though she wasn't sure what about anymore. This guy swamped her senses, from the way he touched her to the way he smelled when he was close to her to the outrageousness of what he was saying.

"You okay?" She tried to answer but it just came out as a whimper, which made him grin. "You'll tell me if it gets to be too much?" She nodded again. As long as he kept the questions to yes or no answers, she might be fine. "Do you want me to warn you what I am going to do first...?"

She nodded again. This was ridiculous and any minute he was going to step back and say he'd made a mistake and had the wrong girl. Except he didn't; instead, he ran the tip of his nose along the shell of her ear, ending with a chaste kiss on her earlobe. She sighed *again* and saw him smile out of the corner of her eye.

As he moved in, she felt a growl rise up her throat.

"Oh, growling is not something you want to start with me, miss. Growling demands something with a little more zing." He moved around behind her.

Dammit, why had she said he couldn't use his hands? Because right now, she wanted his arms around her like she wanted air. She felt his breath on the back of her neck before his lips made contact. Then his tongue tasted her skin for just a second. "So sweet. I'm going to need more of a taste."

Her head dropped forward of its own accord and he pressed up against her back. She felt his nose slide along her skin, then his breath and lips again and then his teeth. Gently he sucked on the band of muscle running down the side of her neck, and then more firmly.

Oh God, he was marking her as his and the thought sent a bolt of desire to her core and made her body pulse. She felt her nipples harden to knots and suddenly her clothes all felt too tight. She wanted to tear at them to get them off her. As if he understood how she felt, he asked her to undo the top button of her shirt. She would still be covered and appropriate. She hadn't realized she had even done it till she felt him slide her collar over and start the same slow torture—skin, breath, lips, teeth—over and over till she was ready to scream. When she was panting, he moved to the front of her. She knew she must have looked crazed but if he didn't kiss her right now she was going to stop breathing. She could feel the first deep rumblings of an orgasm and her eyes went wide with the realization.

"Sweetness, I'm going to kiss you now."

"Oh God, yes." As soon as it was out of her mouth, she wished she could suck it back in. But he didn't laugh at her. He didn't even give her an "I told you so" smile. His smile was sweet and a little shy, just like his kiss started out and then it morphed into something else. Mimi blinked her eyes when she realized the kiss changed because she was kissing him back. Her arms were locked around his neck; her pelvis was rocking against his with the contractions inside her. Her knees did buckle then and he caught her around her waist without breaking the kiss. They just stood there, tasting each other like they each held the secret of life. Finally she came back to herself and started laughing.

"You taste like honey and lemon, and beer," she finally managed to say to him. His eyes were kind of sleepy-looking now and she flushed when he raised an eyebrow at her. "Fine, you win." Now he had a big grin on his face.

"That is the best thing I've heard all day!" His joy was contagious and she started grinning, too. "Come meet my buddy and you can give me your address where I can pick you up." She shouldn't but she trusted him. It was probably the endorphins buzzing around her system, but he'd put them there so what the hell. They navigated the crowd around the dance floor but if he hadn't been holding her hand she wouldn't have moved.

Frankly, she was astonished she could walk at all and was happy when Eric slid into a booth and pulled her in after him.

"Mimi, this is Steve. Steve, Mimi."

"You're the accountant."

Steve gave her a weird look.

"I didn't realize it was tattooed on my forehead but yeah. I guess you are Cinderella?"

Mimi blushed but Eric jumped in to cover for her. "I told them you were an accountant, mostly because her frienemy was being a pain. She's the hot blonde over there."

Steve smirked. "Yeah, thanks for saving me from that. Don't suppose you picked up any beers while you were up there?"

Eric grinned at her and said, "Nope, just a smokin' hot woman." Her mouth dropped open and she pushed at him. He just wrapped one of those long arms of his around her and pulled her closer to him. He reached under her hair and started playing with the little curls at the back of her neck. She fought the urge to lean into him but boy, was it hard. With the two drinks in her and a public orgasm, she was feeling very cuddly and sleepy. *Mmm...cuddling up with Eric would be heaven or even Rose... Oh shoot!*

"I've got to get home to Rose! Here, take down my address and phone and you can let me know when you want to go out on that date." She gave him her info and he gave her his cell number and she hightailed it out of there. Rose was not going to be very happy with her at all. Mimi just hoped she wouldn't destroy something again.

"So dude? Sounds like she's got a kid already. There goes your fairy tale."

Eric thought for a moment. He hadn't figured on a kid. She definitely wasn't married; he'd kissed her hand enough to check. She seemed young for a kid already and why would she be out on a Thursday night if she had a kid at home? Maybe she just needed to blow off steam and was planning to leave when he had shown up. Now he felt bad about keeping her here and the games he played with her. Hmm, a step-kid? What would that be like? Someone he could teach to skate, do art projects with, play video games. Nah, she had said the kid's name was Rose so probably not video games; maybe he could lure her over to the dark side. He smiled. "Nope, I think it is just a different fairy tale.

Besides, your sister has a kid and she's younger than Mimi."

"Yeah, and you know why. Changing the subject. Another round?"

"Sure."

Chapter Two

Her phone buzzed with a text. *Hey Cinderella-*

She ducked her head to hide her blush and her grin. *Hey 2 U too-*

What R U doing?-

Sitting in a meet U?-

Waiting.-

4 what?-

You.-

Mimi groaned; this guy was such a corny sweetheart, he couldn't be real. Gerry turned and looked at her. "Client," she whispered back. *Lunch?-* was the next text that came up on her phone.

Can't :(-

How's Rose?-

Now it was her turn to look confused, but it was sweet he asked.

Good, Playful-

C U Fri.-

Can't wait- She turned off her phone before she got any pinker. Gerry and one of the account guys were looking at her funny now. Well, they could just stew; she didn't have to tell them anything.

***

Eric had walked around all week with a smile on his face. He couldn't remember the last time he was this happy. He had set up the perfect date for him and Mimi; he just needed to take care of one detail.

"Steve, your sister still have the scooter you gave her in college?"

"Yeah. I think it's in her garage."

"Any chance of borrowing it?"

"Okay, now I know you're nuts. What the hell do you want with an old scooter when you have two sports cars and a kick-ass motorcycle?"

"I need it for my date."

"Are you kidding me? Most women would drop their panties just for a ride in one of your cars. And you are going to take her out on an old beat-up scooter?"

Eric grinned to himself. Mimi wasn't like most women. He'd suspected it when he met her the first time and then again in the bar. The text messages back and forth all week as they were getting to know each other better confirmed it. She was sweet in a way the women he usually hung out with would have laughed at. There wasn't a cool, aloof bone in her body and he wanted to cheer because of it. She didn't play games, heck, not even hard to get. She was truly an old-fashioned girl and he wanted to take her on a sweet old-fashioned date.

Watching her catch fire in the bar had turned him on like none of the women he had ever had sex with. God, he couldn't wait to have her laid out beneath him. He just needed to take it real slow. He'd been careful not to overwhelm her too much. She'd probably freak when she got a look at him but if he explained, talked her through it, maybe it wouldn't be so bad.

"Can you call your sister and see if she's home? I'll grab one of the team vans and go pick it up today. It might need a tune-up."

Steve just shook his head.

"I'll call her. You are insane, you know that, right? Hey, if you are going out there anyway can you drop off some graphics for the website to her?"

"Sure. So is this a new line in my job description? Delivery guy?"

"Shut up. The last time you got a date out of it, so I wouldn't complain."

"You know, buddy, you sound kind of tense. Maybe you need to get out of the office more?"

"'Fuckin' smart ass." Steve winged a whiteboard eraser at him but Eric ducked behind the door.

"Missed me! You just need a woman of your own."

"She isn't yours yet, smart ass, and you are playing a dangerous game. Talk to me after she knows the real you."

"That's just it. For once a woman is getting to know the real me and not that asshole Rik Toil."

"Suit yourself, but this has huge potential for disaster."

"Nah, it'll be fine."

***

Eric pulled up in front of the tidy little
bungalow in the old residential neighborhood.
The house looked a lot like its owner: sweet,
stable, welcoming. He wiped his palms on his
jeans. Damn, he couldn't believe he was this
nervous. It was just a date. Except he couldn't
remember the last time he'd had a real old-
fashioned date, just him and the woman he
wanted to be with. The last few years it was like
he traveled with an entourage; this felt way
different. Looking in the mirror, he took off his
helmet and shook his hair out. He pulled his tie
out from where he'd tucked it so it wouldn't flap
in the wind as he was driving over here. He
swallowed hard and wiped his hands off again.
Okay, now he was just making himself crazy. *Just
go to the damn door, Tolland!* He blew out a deep
breath and laughed at himself. He hadn't been
this nervous when he'd taken out his first million
dollar loan.

He knocked on the door and heard Mimi
wrestling with something and then a door shut.
Finally, she opened the door for him and his
breath caught in his chest. She looked amazing
and he wanted to scoop her up in his arms, walk
inside and slam the door on the world behind
him. She had a red skirt on that made her look

curvy as hell and then there were those long legs
of hers. The blouse was simple with a pretty
collar that somehow made you want to kiss her
cheeks. The blouse was white and covered in
cherries. She had put her hair up in some kind of
twist thing that made it smooth in back but then
the front was a cascade of curls. His sisters
would have killed for those curls. She had tied a
scarf around her neck and cocked the knot to the
side. He managed to check the urge to see if his
love bite was still on the back of her neck. Didn't
matter; she was getting another one before the
night was out, that was for sure.

"You look amazing."

"I don't." She stopped and ducked her head;
when she looked up, she started again.
"Thanks."

"Good girl. You need to get used to
compliments, sweet thing, because I intend on
giving you more than you know what to do
with." She just blushed and smiled back at him.
"Do you need anything else?"

"No, I have everything." She held up a little
purse. She went to step past him and he slid his
arm around her waist.

"Not so fast." He leaned forward and gave her
a quick peck on the lips. He watched as her eyes

went soft and her breathing hitched. "Now you won't be surprised when I do that later."

She laughed at him.

"Really, at this point you're worried I'd turn you down? Even after, um, what you managed to do at the bar?"

"Maybe you forgot."

She smirked at him now.

"Not likely."

Yeah, okay, he had a very self-satisfied look on his face now. Tonight was going to be good.

"Oh, I forgot to tell you we are traveling in style tonight." He held his hand out to the little Italian scooter.

"Yikes!"

"Don't worry. I've got a helmet for you."

"Oh, that isn't the problem."

"Then what...I don't understand."

"Um, I can't exactly ride sidesaddle on that and this skirt is too narrow to..."

"So just hitch it up a little." They walked over to the scooter and he straddled it. Mimi untied the scarf from her neck and tied it around her hair. She went from cute to sexy Italian siren in a heartbeat. Next, she shimmied her skirt up a little and tried to get on. No luck, so she pulled her skirt higher and he got a good look at her legs, along with the lace of the top of her silk stockings and the lacy garter belt clips. Thank God she slid in behind him or she would have had a really uncomfortable ride with his erection poking her in the back. He managed a fairly subtle groan before he handed her a helmet and put his on. Then he kicked the scooter into gear and off they went.

Mimi's legs were shaking when Eric stopped the scooter. Feeling her thighs wrapped around his made her think of being pressed against him in the bar. Hell, she was never going to make it through this date without just begging him to take her to bed. As weirdly good as it was having him give her an orgasm without even taking her clothes off, she couldn't help but think it would have been so much better skin to skin. He got off the scooter and turned to help her off. Except he was just staring at her and sort of half growling, half groaning under his breath. She looked down to see that her skirt had ridden up higher during the ride and he was staring at her stockings and garters. She had a flash of what she must look like: black heels, pale stockings and lingerie, red skirt pushed up, straddling the scooter. She

almost started laughing. So that was the appeal
of those tire company calendars.

She swung her legs over the side and fixed
her skirt, which seemed to break the spell Eric
was under.

"So what is this place?" It looked like they
were in front of a house not unlike hers, except
this place was filled with people and loud music.
There were a bunch of people hanging out on
the porch, smoking and talking.

"Come see. You should like this." He grabbed
her hand and pulled her through the crowd on
the porch and into the house. Now that they
were inside, she could hear the music properly
and realized it was rockabilly and swing. She
also noticed the house had little in the way of
furniture and what would have been the front
parlor was functioning as a bar. Most of the
other rooms were being used as dance floors for
the combo in the back room. She grabbed onto
Eric's arm so she didn't lose him in the crush of
people. The people on the dance floor were
amazing to watch. Guys were throwing their
girls in the air and spinning them around their
backs. *Oh God! Eric didn't expect her to do that, did
he?* Those girls were tiny; cue the dancing
elephant worries.

Eric slid behind her and wrapped his arms around her waist. She closed her eyes and held her breath for a second. This, just standing here like this, felt so good.

"Come on, let's dance."

Her heart stopped beating. She was going to make a fool of herself.

"Are you serious? I can't do that!"

"Neither can I. Look, there are other people doing tamer stuff." She followed where he was pointing and on the edges of the dance floor there were other couples dancing but in a much more restrained fashion. *Well, at least no one was getting tossed in the air!*

"I brought you here to dance, but if I'm going to make a fool of myself dancing, I want to be able to touch you," Eric said in her ear, which made her turn to look at him. He took the opportunity to kiss her again. *Well, when he put it like that.* The music did make her want to dance.

"Okay, but let's go over with the tamer crowd." They didn't want to cut through the dance floor so they wove their way through the other rooms to go around. In one of the back bar areas, Mimi ran smack into a guy.

"Sorry!" she yelled and tried to step around him.

"Now where do you think you're going?" He blocked her path and grabbed her arm. She was so surprised, she just looked at his hand holding her wrist for a second. Eric looked at her to see why she had stopped. She just smiled at him and then turned to the guy who was still hanging on to her.

"I said I was sorry; now let go of my arm." He was a big guy, bigger than her and he probably outweighed her by a good eighty pounds. He'd also had too much to drink. *Oh fun!*

"I want a kiszz." *Oh good, now he was slurring his words.* His friends had started to notice what was going on and started laughing. She was getting ticked off.

"And I said I want you to let go of me. If I have to say it again, you have only yourself to blame."

The idiot just started laughing at her. She took a deep breath. She broke his hold and flipped her wrist, grabbing his thumb and jamming it back. He dropped to his knees. When he put his other hand on the ground, she casually placed her heel in the center of it and transferred some of her weight to it. He started blubbering before he even fully registered what had happened. "I said I wanted you to let go of me."

"'Fuckin' bitch. My arm, you're gonna break my arm. I should..." His friends cut him off, realizing too late this wasn't fun and games anymore.

"Lady, we'll get him out of here." She put a little more pressure on his thumb and tears welled in his eyes. "He won't come near you again, we swear!" She let him up and walked away. The crowd in the room parted to let her through like she was Moses parting the sea.

Eric ran up behind her in the next room.

"What the hell was that?" He must have seen how shaky she was and put his arm around her. "Are you okay?" She shouldn't but she just curled into him and hid her face in the crook of his neck. He held her like that till she pulled back. She smiled and tried to make a joke of it.

"Oh, you know, happens all the time."

"I can believe you bring men to their knees, sweet thing, but not usually like that. What you did was fucking amazing. One minute, he was standing there holding your wrist and the next you dropped him like a sack of garbage. And the..." She waited for him to finish but he

couldn't seem to pull it together. Great. Now he
was speechless.

"Could we just go dance?"

"Are you going to show me that sometime?"

"Eugh, fine! I thought this was a date?"

"Oh, it is most definitely a date but here I was
thinking you were like some fairy princess and
you've been hiding a warrior." He leaned into her
and she could see his eyes had turned the same
green they did when she'd been mauling him at
the bar last week. "The combination of lady-like
and femme fatale is hot as hell," he whispered in
her ear. *He was turned on?* He wasn't horrified
that she had knocked the stuffing out of some
guy. That she wasn't some delicate little flower?
She ducked her head to hide her confusion. She
felt his fingers skate along her neck and then
down her chin. He held her chin lightly and
pulled her up to look him in the face. "Hot as
hell," he whispered and then lowered his head to
kiss her. The kiss left no doubt he was talking
about her and left no air in her lungs. When he
pulled away, he looked as shaken as she felt. This
was a first date, for crying out loud! This did not
happen, well, not to her, anyway; she was no
delicate romance novel heroine.

He tugged on her hand. "Let's dance." He pulled her into the room they were headed for. The music changed to a slow song just as they entered the room. *Thank God!* After that kiss, her legs were feeling like jelly and having to walk almost seemed like too much of an effort. He pulled her into his arms and held her close. She laid her head on his shoulder and felt him sigh. He smelled so delicious: citrus, pine, some kind of exotic spice, and male. Now it was her turn to sigh.

She let her fingers explore the bands of muscle in his back. He had the kind of body you get from yoga or rock climbing. Long, lean muscle ran from his waist to his shoulder blades. He looked like he could be quick and lethal, more cheetah than tiger. Thinking about him as a big cat made her remember the love bite he'd given her on the back of her neck and she stumbled against him.

"Sorry."

"You can get closer to me anytime you want." Now he started exploring her back, or at least her backside. She bit the inside of her cheek to keep from laughing. One minute, he was so overwhelmingly sexual and the next he acted like some shy high school boy, like right now.

"Hey, where are those hands going?"

"Uh, I...Shit." She could feel the heat of his blush and giggled into his neck. Maybe it was the adrenaline from the earlier confrontation or just his sudden awkwardness but she started nibbling his neck. She never took the initiative. This guy made her want to take chances, which terrified her. She was Mimi the Meek, at least that is what her parents and Audi had called her. It was the nail in the coffin. She looked big and sturdy on the outside but really she was the one who got picked on and her five-foot-three "big" sister would go tackle the kids that had been picking on her. As an adult, she had learned to stand up for herself some but taking chances, doing the unexpected, was still not her thing.

She lifted her head from his shoulder and smiled at him. She watched as his face went from grim to grin. "Just wanted to prepare myself, that's all."

"You're fresh." His hands had moved back to her waist but as he said it he slid one down and pinched her ass. Then he laughed at the hitch in her breath and the flash of her eyes.

"Hey! Remember, I'm dangerous." She mock glared at him. He gave her another quick kiss. *Oh Lord, this man liked to kiss.*

"More than you know, sweet Mimi."

She could have stayed wrapped in his arms all night but the music ultimately changed to something faster. Eric pushed her away from him and caught her hands. She almost took out two couples. *Damn dancing elephant.* She wished she could make herself smaller, although in all the years she had tried to, it had never succeeded. Still, it didn't stop her from trying. He hauled her up against him while pushing their arms out to the sides. Again they almost whacked a couple in the head. She wanted to hide.

"Wow, it is really crowded in here," Eric yelled over the music. *Was he crazy?* It was because she was so big and awkward they kept getting banged into. She managed to make it through a couple more songs until he spun her out and she stepped on some tiny girl. She apologized but the girl had yelled at her and she wanted to take off running. She apologized even more and then darted for the porch. She desperately needed some air.

She had been leaning over the porch railing, sucking in air, when Eric came up behind her.

"Wow, she was pretty bitchy."

"What? I stepped on her; I'm lucky I didn't crush her! I'm such a clumsy..." He cut her off with a kiss. When he pulled back and she tried to continue her tirade, he put his finger over her lips.

"I'll kiss you all night if I have to. I don't want to hear you tear yourself apart. The place is packed and she was showing off. You apologized and she lit into you worse than she should have. She was obviously the more experienced dancer and should have been able to avoid you. It's no different in skate parks. The more experienced riders look out for the newer ones. Just because you are in a zone doesn't mean you can ignore what is going on around you."

He made it all sound so reasonable, she laughed and he pulled her into his arms again. "Now about kissing you all night..." She looked up at him and watched as his eyes shifted to the deeper blue green. She didn't know what made her look away from them but something distracted her over his shoulder. Mimi saw the pool cue too late to stop it.

"Duck!" She tried to pull him down with her but he was taller and she watched in horror as the stick made contact with his head. He crumpled at her feet. She popped up, grabbed

the cue and snapped it in half over her knee.
Now she had two weapons and she'd be damned
if she was going down without a fight. She
almost choked when she saw who had swung the
thing to begin with.

"Bitch, all my friends are laughing at me." It
was the idiot from the bar earlier. He seemed
more sober but a lot nastier. His friends ran up
and took in the scene: Eric lying in a heap at her
feet, her armed and, she imagined, looking
dangerous, and their friend looking like he
wanted to kill her.

"Oh shit!" One of them stated the obvious.

"No kidding," she yelled back. "You were
supposed to get him home, you jerks." The idiot
took a swing at her with his fist. She blocked
him with the fat end of the cue and poked him in
the ribs with the skinny end. He screamed in
frustration and pain, which finally got his
friends to take some action. They grabbed at
him and managed to hold his arms and
manhandle him off the porch. When they had
him secured, she screamed, "Get him out of here.
I am calling the cops!"

"We will; we're leaving!"

She dropped to her knees and checked on
Eric. He was groggy and had a big egg on his

head but the guy had missed his temple so at least it wasn't as bad as it could have been.

Chapter Three

Eric had a killer headache. Weird, since he didn't remember drinking much. He felt the bed shift next to him and he smiled without opening his eyes. Mmm, Mimi. Just the thought of her in bed with him made his body wake up. Except he couldn't remember what they had done last night. That was definitely not like him. He felt warm puffs of air on his neck and his heart rate kicked up. He wanted to move but he felt so sluggish. *Must be the hangover.* Which was why he didn't ever drink more than a beer or two; last night must have gotten pretty wild. So why didn't he remember it? Now he felt a warm tongue give a little lick to the back of his neck.

Okay, somebody wakes up on the frisky side of the bed. He took a deep breath and forced himself to roll over; opening his eyes was still beyond him, though. *Hmm, warm and soft.* His body curled against hers automatically. He got a hand loose and reached for her and felt fur. *Must be one of those fur throw things like the decorator put in his place.* He never used it but then he was probably hogging the covers last night. The thought of Mimi wrapped in fur was much more interesting. He was just exploring that idea when a large, wet tongue licked him from chin to forehead. His eyes sprung open now. He stared into the biggest brown eyes he'd ever seen and got a face full of dog breath.

"You moose, let him alone." The dog got off the bed and Mimi sat down next to him. "How do you feel?"

Ridiculous was the correct answer but he didn't want to explain he'd been thinking of her next to him.

"Like it must have been one hell of a party. My head is killing me."

"It wasn't the party. You ended up with a concussion. Do you remember anything from last night?"

Now he was really confused.

"Did I fall or something?"

"No. Do you remember the guy grabbing me in the bar?" He nodded his head yes and then winced. "You probably shouldn't move your head much. He showed up when we were on the porch. He came after me but hit you instead. I ended up calling a friend who is a paramedic." Eric swallowed hard against the feelings rushing through him. He hadn't been able to protect her when he should have and she had to call some other guy to help her out.

"Tina examined you and said since we didn't know your insurance situation, I could just take you home and watch you. She also said you should stay put for a couple of days. So no getting out of bed except to use the bathroom. Look at me." She took his head in her hands and pulled one of his eyes open farther. "Okay, your pupils are reacting okay, so she said you can eat a little. I've got soup going on the stove; you want some?"

"Hold up. I'm still trying to understand what happened. Some guy punched me?"

"No, he hit you in the side of the head with a pool cue."

"The paramedic was a girl."

She looked at him like he was nuts and crossed her arms over her chest.

"I don't see what difference it makes but yes, Tina is a woman. She is just as capable as any man..."

"Relax, I didn't mean it like that. I didn't like the idea of you calling a guy—just me being a possessive jerk. I'm happy it was a girl. So Rose was okay with me sleeping here?" He knew how he felt about her but he didn't want to put her in an awkward position with her daughter. She was giving him a strange look now.

"Rose loves when we have company. She'd probably slobber all over you if you let her."

Huh? He had assumed the kid would be older.

"How old is she?"

"I don't know exactly; they figured she was around three when I got her and I've had her about two years."

"No one knew when her birthday was?" He was shocked. Maybe she had adopted her from a different country but then wouldn't they have at least given her a specific birthday?

"It wasn't like her mother could tell us."

Her mother was dead! This was sounding more and more gruesome.

"I should properly introduce the two of you. Rosie, c'mere girl." A huge dog lumbered in. The possessor of the soulful brown eyes and wet tongue he'd encountered earlier. He looked from the dog to Mimi and back. Then he started cracking up; it hurt like hell and he ended up holding his head but he couldn't stop.

"Are you losing it? She's just a dog."

"I...I thought you had a kid. I was all set to try to win you and your daughter over."

Now she started laughing.

"Sorry to disappoint you but it is just me, well and Rose. Trust me, she has enough issues to be a teenage girl."

Funny, part of him <u>was</u> disappointed, not a lot, but he'd been kind of looking forward to being part of a family. The thought stopped his laughter. Yeah, with Mimi he could actually imagine a family and doing all the hokey things his parents did with them that, if he was completely honest, he kinda missed. *Maybe they could borrow a kid. Steve's niece maybe? Hmm, thirteen-year-old girl. Er maybe not, or at least not yet.* Rose gave him another big lick.

"Okay you, can you get your master to give me a kiss?"

"You're supposed to be convalescing, not playing kissy-face."

"Who says I'm playing, and why can't you kiss it and make it better?" He knew he was being goofy but she brought out the big dumb geek in him.

"I don't think that is such a great idea."

"Why not?"

"If I kiss you then you will think I should get in bed with you, and if I get in bed with you, then you will think we should have sex. We are not having sex, so I think it is safer to stay right where I am."

He scowled. He couldn't disagree with her logic but he wasn't about to let her get away quite that easily. He reached out and twirled some of her hair around his finger and very gently tugged her closer. He watched as her eyes got wide. They seemed to be glued to his shoulder. He glanced down and realized the knock on the head must have really rattled him because he hadn't thought about being almost naked. Shit, well what was done was done; it wasn't like he could take them off. If she lost it with this, she was really going to freak later.

"Mimi? What are you thinking?"

"You have a lot of tattoos."

"Two half-sleeves and a full torso but you knew that if you took my shirt off last night."

"It was dark and I didn't get a good look." Damn, in his world what he'd done to himself wasn't all that unusual. Hell, most people admired the work and left it at that. He'd been aware of only going to a couple of artists so that there was a certain harmony to the work and not just a lot of random pieces.

"Does it freak you out? I mean, I'd hate for you to think less of me..."

"Oh, no, nothing like that! It's just, it must have been expensive, I mean for a guy who works as a courier, I mean."

He bit the inside of his cheek to keep from laughing. It was kind of sweet her, being concerned about his profligate ways.

"I was a lot younger then." She was still staring at him with an odd look on her face; she wasn't freaked but obviously damn curious. "Did you want a closer look?"

"Oh...I didn't mean...Could I?"

He pushed the comforter down to his waist and lay back with his arms behind his head. "I'm all yours." She just about pounced on him. She traced along a koi fish done by the artist that specialized in Irezumi, the Japanese style of tattooing, and then followed it to the chrysanthemum the same artist had done. If she liked those she'd love the dragon the guy did on his back. Next, she moved to the mermaid. He thought he saw her eyes light up a little.

"Yeah, she looks a lot like you." Her hands on him were making it hard to breathe. "'Course, you're sexier." He had to touch her but he had the feeling that if he tried to, she'd bolt. She was such a contradiction. On the one hand, she could drop a guy to his knees with a flick of her wrist and on the other, well, she could bring him to his knees just by leaning forward the way she was now. Her hip was warm and soft against his side and she was leaning over him with a hand braced on the other side of him. He quelled the urge to bump her arm so she would fall across him. As much as he wanted to feel her against him, she was skittish and wouldn't appreciate feeling cornered. He unfolded one of his arms and she moved her inspection to his shoulder and the tribal work he had there. She was so engrossed she didn't flinch when he curled his fingers in her hair. She actually looked surprised when he tugged on it.

"Oh, sorry, this stuff always fascinated me."

"I don't mind you looking at me like that."
She blushed crimson. "I got the idea of doing the
full cover from the Yazuka. I'm not into the
crime part but the look was pretty compelling to
a guy who..." His voice trailed off. *How was she
going to take this?* They hadn't slept together yet.
The fact that he'd already given her an orgasm
while she was fully dressed didn't really count, at
least not for him.

"That, what?"

"That was a painfully shy geek artist, at least
around girls." It was half an answer and true, at
least in the beginning. It was way too early to
explain he'd become a dom to get over his
shyness or how even in that world he was
something of a freak because he only stuck to
pretty low-level stuff: sensation play, more silk
than leather, although leather did have it's own
rewards. He hadn't been able to get beyond
thinking about the harder stuff happening to
either of his sisters. Even if it was consensual.
For him, it was about the power exchange more
than anything he actually did.

"You don't strike me as shy now." He laughed
and she did, too. No, he wasn't shy anymore. He
couldn't resist any longer and bumped her arm
with his hip, making her sprawl across him. He

leaned forward and took the kiss he'd been craving. She tasted of coffee, which may have been why his stomach growled. She pulled back quickly. "But evidently you are hungry. I'll get that soup for you and I probably shouldn't but do you want some toast with it?"

He nodded his head like a kid who'd been asked if he wanted cookies. "And even half a cup of coffee, please, so I don't go into complete withdrawal." He was not above begging. She just smirked at him.

"Get some food in your stomach first. How bad does your head hurt?"

"Like I was hit with a pool cue."

"Cute. You stay there."

He didn't do well with forced inactivity so he followed her out to the kitchen after he'd found his jeans.

Well, Audi had been telling her she needed a man in her bed. Somehow, though, Mimi didn't think this was quite what she meant. She had watched him sleep most of the night from the chair next to the bed, terrified he'd go into a coma or something despite what Tina had told her. It would have been just her luck to finally meet some amazing guy and have him die in her bed without him ever having touched her. She smiled at the thought of finally getting to run her hands over him. She had been intrigued by his body art last night when Tina was helping get him into her bed but this morning was sexy as all hell. Running her fingers over the designs, feeling the muscles move under his skin had been subtly erotic. Like it was him but not him. She shook her head.

He was so out of her league. The looks, the skateboarding, the tats, even the couple of hoops in each ear. He made her mouth water and he was all wrong for her. She wasn't the wild one: no tattoos, one little hole in each ear. She'd done dance, not skateboarding, but then she had outgrown it, literally. She wasn't ugly but she didn't kid herself that she had any kind of edge. She was fascinated by the whole body art, hardcore lifestyle but she looked down at herself and snorted. She had never seen a girl who looked like her in any of the magazines she snuck glances at. He might like the novelty of her but sooner or later, he'd realize she would never fit in with his life.

As much as it hurt at the time, the idiots at work were right: she was no skater's girl. He had said he started as a geeky artist. Well, if she

couldn't really date him, maybe she could help
him get the word out about his art. A noise
behind her made her turn around and her mouth
dropped open; she recovered and snapped it
shut. There he was in all his glory. His hair
hanging in his face, which somehow brought out
those teal eyes of his. Then there was his body,
which was at the moment only half dressed.
There was no mistaking the power in his long
legs. He looked centered and coiled like a spring.
She had seen the same thing in some of the stick
fighting masters she had trained with but they
tended to be shorter and stockier. Eric's muscles
were leaner and made her want to run her hands
over them like she had his chest. *Mmm, that chest.*
He was one of those guys that naturally didn't
have any chest hair, which made the artwork
stand out better. Maybe that was part of why
he'd done it. It couldn't have been easy to be
eighteen or nineteen and feel like you were still
waiting for something to tell you that you were a
man now. Her eyes dropped to his waist and her
breath caught in her throat. He'd left the top
button undone, which highlighted the fine gold
hair marking a line toward...

"Soup smells good."

She snapped her eyes up to his and the crinkles on the corners told her he hadn't missed any of her very thorough inspection. When she tried to stare at the floor, she caught sight of his bare feet. She had never thought of men's feet as sexy in the least but his were perfect. Whatever that meant, she felt addled; it had to be from not enough sleep. That had to be why she wanted to curl herself around him and purr. Right— elephants don't curl up with anyone, not even other elephants.

"You are supposed to be in bed."

"I got lonely. What am I supposed to do in bed all weekend? I hate television except when the X Games are on but you don't even have one in there." She hated television, too, which wasn't great considering her career choice but then she usually handled print accounts. Maybe that was why.

"You're supposed to be resting. Why don't you go scan my iPod and see if there is anything you like? I also have some CDs on the shelf in the living room. Take a look while I get your soup dished up." She was just putting the pain reliever on the table when he walked back in.

"You have pretty varied musical taste."

"Is that your polite way of saying you didn't find anything you liked?" He had a couple of CDs in his hands so he must have chosen a few things.

"I found something; actually it was surprising for a couple of reasons. How did you get studio cuts of the Harridans? They're one of my favorite bands and even I don't have these. The interesting thing is none of your other music seems like you'd be a Harridans fan."

Damn! Why did she keep those out? She loved her sister's music, even if she didn't adore the whole genre, and part of it was sheer pride. Now he was going to go all fanboy unless...she could just lie, a little, more of an omission than an outright fib. *Okay, she was rationalizing.* He was all wrong for her and it shouldn't matter if he liked Audi but... There was the weird pull she felt and the words were out of her mouth before she could stop them.

"I have a friend at the recording studio; they thought I could use them in a commercial. I liked them, though, so I hung on to the discs."

"Yeah, they are great. Have you seen them in concert?"

She and her sister had shared a bedroom growing up, so she'd had front row seats to the early years. The image of her pixie of a sister

prancing around on her bed belting out Joan
Jett still made her laugh.

"Once." *Or a few dozen times.* "I might be able
to see if my friend could get you tickets and
passes the next time they are in town." He'd be
over her by then, so it shouldn't hurt so much if
he decided to go after Audi. She'd fit in better in
his world, anyway.

"Oh, um, yeah, that would be great." He was
talking to his feet now. Had she embarrassed
him? Damn, maybe he thought he'd have to take
her.

"I could probably get four if you want to take
three of your friends." Now he looked at her
strangely. Rose picked that moment to lumber in
and they both seemed grateful for the
distraction.

"So what breed is she?" he asked as he
rubbed her ears. Her dog was not unlike her and
Rose moaned and groaned in pleasure as he pet
her. *Way to play hard to get!*

"I got her from a rescue so I'm never going to
be entirely sure but there is a lot of herd dog in
her. But based on her size and coloring, probably
St. Bernard, too. When I first got her, she was
afraid of her own shadow. No one knew what her
history was but it couldn't have been good.

We've worked on a lot of trust issues." She reached over and scratched Rose's head while the dog's tongue hung out of the side of her mouth. Eric slid his hand over hers and lifted it to his lips. Her whole body buzzed with anticipation but she shut it down quick.

"You should eat before everything gets cold." She watched as his eyes dimmed slightly but he smiled at her.

"So what kind of things did you do to rebuild her trust?" he said as he pulled out the chair where she had put his food. She sat down next to him.

"Some herd dog breeds are bred to work with one master and bond to that person. If the person abuses them, they end up sort of PTSD. Rose wouldn't make eye contact, her tail was always between her legs—those are classic signs of trauma in a dog. So we spent a lot of time together, just stroking her, letting her get used to me. I made sure she had a safe place she could always go." She started laughing, remembering how much Rose had hated crate training in the beginning. "Though she wasn't so sure about it at first. I made sure we had a routine she could count on. As she got more used to me, I started adding other things. It was so sad in the beginning. She didn't play, would cower from everyone—even other dogs, like she had no idea what they were." She looked down at Rose, lying on her back, begging for a belly rub. "As you can see, she now thinks we are all here to cater to her every whim."

"So if I work on your trust issues, you'll beg for me to rub your belly?"

She gasped but he was smiling at her.

Dammit, why did she have to be so attracted to him?

"I don't have any trust issues."

"No? Okay, so when we're done here, you and I are going to curl up in bed and sleep."

"Yeah, right! Just sleep?"

"Yeah, because from the circles under your eyes, I don't think you slept at all last night. Did you?"

She looked down at her lap. "Not much. I was afraid I wouldn't wake up to check on you."

"Okay, last night you took care of me. Now I'm going to take care of you and to prove you don't have any trust issues, you are going to let me."

She gritted her teeth till she realized he was laughing at her.

"Fine."

"Fine. I promise I'll be a gentleman. I'm serious; I want to wrap myself around you and sleep." He washed down the pills with some water and stood up. He held his hand out to her and she just stared at him. *Why was he doing this?* He was just going to leave after he got tired or bored with her. "You all set? I mean, did you want to change or anything?" She was wearing yoga pants and a T-shirt along with a bra and panties; she supposed changing into armor wouldn't really do any good since the only thing that really needed protecting was her heart.

"I'm good."

"You're sure?"

"Yeah, can we just get this over with?"

He laughed at her.

"After we work on trust, maybe we'll work on a little enthusiasm. Come on, this will be good." He held on to her hand and led her to her bedroom. He fooled around with her music for a second and then Jason Mraz's "Butterfly" started playing softly. She groaned inside. This song was one of her favorites because it was so frankly sensual. She used to dream about someone feeling like that about her. She watched as he climbed into her bed. Suddenly, her queen-size bed looked minuscule with him sprawled across it. He pulled the covers over himself and then held them up for her to get under.

"You're going to sleep in your jeans?"

"Not usually but um, if I want to keep my promise, I think I should. Coming?"

She swallowed hard and got into her bed. She had placed her back to him and he folded her in a cocoon of his arms and the quilt. It felt so good, she wanted to cry and her body stiffened against him to ward off giving in to what would just inevitably be hurt.

"See, that wasn't so hard." She felt his hand rubbing her back as he lulled her to relax. She snapped to attention when she felt her bra give way.

"What are you doing?"

"I have two sisters and you cannot tell me you think these things are comfortable. I know enough about them to know this one has some hard wires or whatever in it. Come on, off it goes."

"You want me to take off my shirt?"

He snorted. "If I thought you wouldn't bolt, hell yeah. But let's work on one thing at a time. My sisters can do this thing where they take off their bra without getting undressed. I'm assuming you can too."

She smirked at him and sat up. She reached behind her and re-hooked her bra.

"Mimi, there is no way you are going to be able to sleep like that."

He was right, of course. But she wasn't going to be able to sleep, anyway.

"Eric, I..." How did she just flat out say she didn't want him to see her without a bra? What had the girls said in high school—she was way more than a mouthful? Hell more than a handful even and despite not being thirty yet, she was big and droopy and there was no way she wanted to see that look in his eyes that said, "oh, now you remind me of a cow'."

"Mimi, you said you'd let me take care of you. Are you going back on that?"

Dammit, what did it matter? She was only delaying the inevitable.

"Fine! I don't know why it makes such a difference to you." She reached back and unhooked her bra, pulled her arms out of her T-shirt and then the bra. Finally, while trying to cradle her breasts with one arm, she managed to pull the bra out from below the hem of the shirt. She tossed it on the chair and turned over with her back to him again. "Happy now?"

"Yes and no. I'm happy you'll be more comfortable and more likely to sleep but it is going to be damn uncomfortable keeping my promise." He curled around her again and she felt his erection trapped behind his zipper. Hmm, serves him right, she thought, but then felt bad about it. He was turned on by her; the thought flit like a butterfly in her brain, making her smile. He started whispering things in her ear she could barely hear or understand. His breath and lips drugged her in to relaxing; that was the only explanation for her snuggling up against him more. She didn't balk when he slid his arm under her head or when the arm at her waist moved up to cradle her breasts like she had done. She felt deliciously liquid. "That's it, sleep, sweet angel. I've got you," were the last words she heard as she fell asleep.

Chapter Four

Mmm, she was having the most marvelous dream. Eric was touching her, loving her body, not just having sex with her but making love, slowly, letting her warm up, bringing her up in waves. Nothing had ever felt as perfect as this. Her body tightened, bracing for the coming onslaught; at the first pulse, her eyes fluttered open and she realized she was alone in bed. It wasn't dark but it had to be late afternoon. Her heart was pounding in her chest and her body was still lost in the throes of the dream. She scanned the room almost blindly till she saw him in the chair. Only then did her heart start to unclench. He had his ankle crossed over his other knee, supporting one of her sketch pads. He was still dressed in just the jeans with his hair flopped over his eyes. He was so engrossed in his drawing, he didn't realize she was awake and watching him now. When he finally saw, he smiled at her.

"Afternoon, beautiful."

She sucked in air like she had come from deep under water and blinked a few times to try to rouse her brain. She felt warm and melty from sleep and what seemed to be her body's natural reaction to him.

"Hi." Oh God, her voice sounded breathy and squeaky at the same time. She watched transfixed as he unfolded himself from the chair and knelt on the floor next to the bed. He kissed her like he was having dessert, savoring each nibble and lick. When he finally sat back on his heels, she was reduced to a sighing puddle. She managed to straighten the covers around her and propped herself up on her elbows.

"You don't mind I used some of your supplies, do you?"

"No, it's fine. I've got plenty. What were you drawing?"

His grin got ridiculously wide.

"I think I have a new muse. I've been kind of blocked lately. I don't know how to describe it exactly; there were all these ideas but something was blocking the pipeline. As I was lying there watching you sleep..." He flipped the pad around so she could see what he'd been working on. Some of the bits were studies where he was obviously getting used to the materials and limbering up his hand. Then he started to get into it. There were quick studies of hands and textures as you moved down the page. When he saw that she was looking at the bottom of the page, he flipped to the next. The studies were bigger now, abstract organic curves that made her think of landscapes but sensual and soft. Again, he flipped the page and she gasped.

It was her, even if her face was turned away. Her lower body was facing him and the contours were clear under the quilt. Her shoulders were back against the mattress but her torso wasn't under the covers. Her T-shirt had ridden up, so one nipple was barely visible but it showed off the lower curve of her breast and captured the texture of her skin. It seemed impossible that it could just be pencil. *This is the way a lover sees a woman.*

"Eric..." What did she say? That he made her feel beautiful? That he shouldn't see her like that? She felt all the air leave her lungs and her heart start pounding.

"I'm pretty rusty but..."

"Don't you dare. This is amazing. Don't you dare make it sound like nothing." She looked at him and knew there were tears in her eyes. The woman he'd drawn was sensual in a way she had never allowed herself to feel before but did now, because of how he saw her. She draped her arm around him and he leaned into her. She explored his shoulder with her lips, felt his pulse jump in his neck when she licked across the skin there. She smiled at his groan when she dragged her teeth across the tendons. When she bit down on his earlobe, his breath hissed through his teeth and he pulled away. She felt crazed with desire. Yes, he was all wrong for her, and it wasn't going to go anywhere, but right now she didn't care.

"Hold up." He was panting as hard as she was. *Why did the man still have clothes on?* "I think we need to slow down." He couldn't have cooled her off faster if he had dumped ice water on her. She recoiled from him. He started to lean toward her again.

"No, no, I think you are right. I don't know what I was doing. It was just..."

"Mimi..."

She jumped out of bed and moved away from him.

"You're supposed to be the one in bed, mister. I'm going to throw on a sweater and take Rose for a walk. She must think something is wrong." She was chattering but she couldn't stop. She pulled open two drawers before she found the one with sweaters and pulled out a long cardigan. It was only when she stood up she remembered she didn't have a bra on. The urge to flee was greater than the sense of propriety. A sweater would have to cover it. The minute Rose heard the leash jingle, she came running. Mimi slid on ballet flats and just about ran out the door. When she got to the other side, she stopped and leaned against it, fighting off tears and to catch her breath.

"Idiot! Idiot! Idiot! Fuck." He couldn't have just eased her back, slowed her down and then explained why he wanted a second? She had him so juiced, he couldn't think. So much for his precious control. Shit, now what was he supposed to do? At least she had to come back; it was her house. Maybe he should just 'fess up and tell her everything. *Yeah, like it would help at this point.* She'd probably go out the damn window to get away from him. For a minute there, he'd felt like he was flying, everything was working, and

then he had to fuck it up. *Smooth, Tolland, 'fuckin'
smooth.* She got him so hot, though, and to have
her look at the piece he'd done of her and see it,
really see it...not just as a picture but as how he
felt. Damn, he had forgotten how incredible it
was. The connection was electric. He had to find
a way to make it right. He racked his brain for a
way to make things right, to find a way to get her
to trust him; hell, it was asking too much at this
point to have her love him but maybe there was
still a chance.

He'd figured she would come back when it
started raining, not just the usual Seattle
sprinkle, but a real honest-to-God downpour. He
sat in the front parlor with the sketchpad,
mostly just scribbling, to pass the time. He
looked at his phone and realized she'd been gone
over an hour. Dammit, she had only grabbed a
sweater; she was going to freeze to death. He
only wanted her back here and safe. A noise out
on the porch made him look up and then make a
mad dash to open the door. Rose bounded inside,
dragging Mimi. He didn't know whether to kiss
her or kill the woman. *How could she have stayed
out in this weather?* She was shaking and her
teeth were chattering, she was so cold.

He wrapped himself around her and quickly realized it was not going to be enough. He picked her up. "I don't want to hear a single word out of you, miss." So much for wooing and cajoling her back into his arms. Sometimes you just had to grab the bull by the horns. She was stunned enough that she didn't fight him when he stood her in the bathroom and held her there while he turned the shower on and got it up to temperature. Then he lifted her up again and climbed in with her.

She was still shaking and her lips still had a bluish cast to them. Damn the torpedoes; well, this wasn't how he thought he'd be doing this but nothing else had gone to plan, either. He slid her sweater off her shoulders and dropped it into the tub; next came her T-shirt and her yoga pants. When he reached for the lace panties, his hand got slapped. *Finally!*

"You're dressed. In the shower."

"So were you."

"I was already soaked."

"I noticed. Your lips aren't blue anymore." He knew it was a mistake as soon as the thought appeared in his addled mind but hell, he had a beautiful, nearly naked woman standing in front of him. No jury of his peers would convict him.

He kissed her softly at first but he could feel
himself losing the tight rein on his control again.
When he backed away, her eyes were closed but
she wasn't trying to get away so he kissed her
again and let his hands explore her. His hands
glided over her soft, smooth curves. He let his
fingers coast over her hips and down her ass.
With the flat of his palms, he smoothed over her
back. He never let his lips leave hers till she
pushed him away. He could only stare at her,
panting.

"You're not getting out of here yet. You're
still freezing."

"Fine but I don't think you need to be here,
too." Now that he'd backed off, she was trying to
find some way to cover herself. She finally just
gave up and crossed her arms over her chest.

He started to laugh but caught himself.
Laughing would only earn him a slap across the
cheek.

"See, that is where you are wrong. I grew up
in Boston. I've got lots of experience with
hypothermia."

She snorted.

"I'll bet."

"It's true. I suck at ice-skating and some of
the guys were messing with me and pushed me

through the hole in the ice." He ducked his head to hide the smile at how her expression had changed. You would think she had forgotten all about being naked. "My older sister had to get me out and then she threatened the guys with telling their mothers." He paused for a second. "Yeah, life was definitely not fun for a while. I still can't ice skate." She started laughing. "It's not funny; in Boston that is equivalent to not drinking coffee here." He put his arms around her now and started kissing her shoulder while he rubbed her arms. "Warming up?"

She looked at him with her eyes glazed with desire.

Tolland, don't blow this again, he chastised himself.

"Mimi?"

"Hmm..."

He reached past her to turn off the water and they both stood there, dripping, for a second. He came out of his fog first and reached for the towels on the rack, wrapping her in the bath sheet and gently massaging her scalp with the other to dry her hair. Then he lifted her out and stood her next to him. He was dripping all over the floor and his clothes were sopping wet.

"Oh, you're getting everything wet."

"Sorry. Got another towel?" She nodded yes and pulled one from the closet near the door. "Um, I'll be there in a sec." She didn't move. *O-Kay...* He stripped off his shirt and she got that look on her face like she was starved and he was chocolate. He unbuttoned his jeans and peeked up at her. She gave a little shiver but he didn't think it was from cold this time. He peeled down the waistband and saw her lick her lips. God, if he wasn't already hard as a rock, that would have done it. He almost laughed; she had no idea what she looked like right now and her total lack of awareness was sexy as hell. He turned around and pulled off the jeans. He took a deep breath and pulled off his boxers. *Did she just groan?* He got the towel wrapped around his hips so it would stay put, his erection making itself known.

"Let's get you into bed to finish warming up." His voice sounded like a croak.

"Eric, I don't think..."

"No, you didn't think. Why didn't you just come back when it started pouring? I get that you weren't happy with me but we could have talked about it. You think I pushed you away because I didn't want you?" Okay, giving vent to his frustration was not a smart idea, but at this point he was almost beyond caring. Her obvious desire for him, combined with her jumping out of her skin if he came at her too fast, was making him crazy. "If you had any idea what I want...Right now I want to take you over my knee and spank your stubborn ass but that isn't the kind of guy I am. So, you are going to be a good girl and get into bed and I am going to curse the fact I was raised a gentleman and curl up around you to warm you up. Got it?"

She stood there motionless with her eyes wide, looking lost and vulnerable. He wanted to take it all back, whisper sweet words instead, but despite the obvious omissions in what he had told her about himself, he had been essentially honest. He meant everything he'd just said. He drew himself up to his full height and crossed his arms over his chest. He stared her down for a second and then he barked at her.

"Now!"

She actually yelped and raced out of the bathroom. He just stood there and shook his head. He'd said things were too easy, he'd been bored; well, she sure as hell was the antidote to everything else in his life.

When he got to the bedroom, she had changed into a thick terry cloth robe and her hair was wrapped in the towel turban style. She wouldn't look at him and pointed to a silky kimono at the end of the bed.

"I...Maybe you want to use that till your clothes dry."

"Mimi, look at me." She looked up at him and he almost choked. The woman was so turned on he could see it coming off of her in waves. He deserved sainthood. "We're just going to curl up together. I promise."

"Why?" The sound was torn out of her. Unfortunately, he didn't have an answer for her.

"Mimi, there are things about me...things we haven't talked about."

"Just say it! You don't do fat girls. You don't want me! I'm fine for a little grab and tickle but not to..."

He climbed over the bed and nearly tossed her on it. He managed to check himself and held on to her as he eased her down. His lungs burned with trying to hold himself back.

"You are not fat. I don't ever want you to say that again! Want you? Are you fucking kidding me? What the hell does this feel like to you?" He ground his now painful erection into her abdomen. "Dammit, I have been trying to take it slow because you seem to bolt if I get too close. Mimi, I..." He swallowed hard. If she laughed at

him, he might damn well lose it. "I was trying to
go slow because I wanted to ease you into what I
am, what I'm into. It's not just the tats—it's..."

"You're a vegetarian."

He shook his head. *What the hell?*

"Yeah, but that isn't..." *Random.* "Mimi, I'm
a...dominant."

"Oh, come on!" She struggled to get out from
under him.

"You don't believe me?"

"You have got to be kidding me! I would have
believed you didn't want me but this, God, you
really think I am stupid."

When he growled at her, she stopped
breathing.

"Oh, I am dead serious and I am going to
make a believer out of you, miss."

Her eyes got round and she looked like she
might scream.

"Wh...What are you going to do?"

"First off, I need this." He reached between
them and yanked out her bathrobe belt. As he
pinned her body under his, she watched,
fascinated, as he pulled the tie out. He left it by
her ear and then smoothed his hands up her
arms. As he stared into her eyes, he lifted her
arms above her head and tied them together and

to her headboard. "Mimi, what do you know about this?"

"Just the stuff in those books," she whispered; her breathing was shallow either from fear or arousal.

"So nothing beyond 'laters baby'?"

She nodded yes.

"Okay, well there is a lot more to the lifestyle than that. Different people are into different things. I don't really do pain, to myself or others when I play. I have two sisters and the thought of some guy doing stuff like that to them would make me crazy. I got into this because, as a six-foot-four geek in college, I could barely speak to a girl. The training gave me a confidence I didn't have before. When I knew I could make them crazy with want, I wasn't so scared of talking to them."

"The thing you did in the bar?"

"Yes. That was part of it. God, you were stunning and so receptive. You have no idea how badly I wanted to drag you behind the building and devour you. Nothing I am going to do is going to cause you any pain. You might be a little uncomfortable when I'm teasing you but it will be worth it, I promise. So do you really not believe me?"

She nodded her head yes, slowly.

"Okay, by the time I am done with you, you will understand and either you will be okay with it or never want to see me again. Are you in any pain now? Are your shoulders comfortable enough?" The tiniest nod came back to him. "Are you tied too tight? I don't want to cut off the circulation in your hands."

"No." She was whispering. He leaned down and kissed her like he had in the shower, only this time she whimpered when he pulled away.

"Oh, you are in big trouble, my warrior angel. Are you going to be able to do as I ask or do I need to tie those legs down?"

She shook her head furiously back and forth.

"I'll be good."

He gave her a quick kiss.

"I have no doubt about that. Now I want to explore this luscious body of yours better than I have." He parted her robe as she sucked in a breath. "Mimi, if you've read those books then you know about red/yellow/green..."

"Green! Green, really green."

"Okay. You'll let me know if it changes." She nodded like crazy while biting her lip. He hadn't done anything and she looked ready to expire. "Babe, this is supposed to be fun for both of us.

You look a little tense so I'm going to take things slow. Lots of talking," he whispered in her ear. He unwrapped her hair and fanned it out to dry. "So what I specialize in is called sensation play." She had closed her eyes but there was a little furrow between her eyebrows now that he bent to kiss. "Most BDSM has some level of sensation play. Hmm, wait here a sec." He ran to the freezer and came back to find her wide-eyed again. He held up the ice tray and smiled. "Okay, this is pretty basic. Just some ice cubes. Nothing to be afraid of." She calmed down; obviously she had never had this done to her. He popped one in his mouth and waggled his eyebrows at her, which made her giggle. The giggle died in her throat when he bent and sucked her nipple against the ice cube.

"Oh, shit! Eric!"

He didn't let her go but did look her in the eye now.

She sucked air in through her teeth. Her heart hammered in her chest, even more than it had in the shower. Her nipple felt like it was on fire but with each pull, she could feel her body arch and pulse in time. "Oh, my God! Eric! Please!" What she wanted him to do exactly, she had no idea but her mind was reeling from the sensations. Finally, he released her nipple and she sucked in great gasps of air as he crunched the ice cube.

"So sensation play can be dramatic or as simple as this." He bent over her body and placed kisses down the center till he got to her navel. He dipped his tongue into it and swirled it around. His tongue was cool from the ice but it warmed against her skin quickly. Her body convulsed as she moaned. "Mimi, you are so exquisitely sensitive. I could do this forever."

"Oh, God." She buried her face against her arm. She wasn't going to survive.

"The most important part of any BDSM experience is when the sub gives up their power and completely puts themselves in the dom's hands. How you get there is just technique. There are a lot of women that weren't able to do that with me because I wasn't willing to go to the point of pain with them. Hard-core subs are usually confused by what I want. But you..."

He didn't finish his sentence. He fished another ice cube out of the tray and ran it down her body. She felt a contraction deep inside her and then he painted her navel with it. He left it there and popped another in his mouth. This

time he kissed her. When she felt his fingers on
the inside of her thigh, her mouth opened and he
passed her the melting cube and then followed it
with his tongue. Warmth and cold at the same
time seemed to short-circuit her brain; she
stopped thinking and just felt. The water
dripping down her waist from the cube in her
belly button became just another sensation.

His fingers stroked the inside of her thigh
and then she felt them hook her panties and
drag them down her legs. He stopped for a
second. When she opened her eyes, he was
staring at her mound. She wanted to pull her
legs together but he had his arm wrapped
around one of them.

"You still green?"

She blew out a breath and said yes.

"There are some things that I use that you'll
know from the books." She tensed up. *Here it
comes: he was going to tell her that he like to use a
flogger or, crap, what if he liked a cane?* That was
what they used to punish people in Singapore.
She was about to say red when he put his finger
to her lips. *Had she been broadcasting what was
going on in her head?*

"I'm talking about mechanisms of control. No
orgasms unless I give you permission. That

means, no touching yourself and not allowing anyone else to touch you." He ground that last part through his teeth like the thought made him angry. *Like she would want anyone else at this point?* "I own all of your orgasms, understand?" She nodded yes and buried her face in the sleeve of her robe. All this talking about orgasms was making it hard to concentrate.

"Mimi, look at me." She peeked over at him. He had a very mischievous smile on his face. "I'm going to ask you a question and I want an honest answer. How many times have you gotten off since we met?"

"What? You can't be serious? We...how...oh, hell." She thought about the times in the shower when she had fantasized about what kind of a lover he'd be. The times she had been lying in bed, wishing that it was time for their date already. She was so screwed. "Do dreams count?"

He backed off and then his smile got even wider.

"You had dreams about me that got you off?" She nodded; admitting it out loud was too much to bear. "Oh, yeah, they definitely count."

Shit. "Fine, eight."

His eyebrows shot up.

"You had eight dreams about me?"

"No, two dreams that...I had other dreams about you that didn't, um, end up like that. Then there were six other times when..." She blushed even darker than she already was.

"When? Finish the sentence."

Damn him! She could feel her whole body turning pink from embarrassment.

"You are evil. Fine, that I got myself off thinking about you touching me or making love to me in the last week."

"How does the real thing compare?"

"It wasn't even in the same ballpark."

"Okay, so you owe me for eight orgasms I missed out on. To pay me back, you are going to climax for eight minutes straight."

Her mouth fell open.

"That isn't even possible."

"Oh, my little warrior angel, not only is it possible, you will get to the point where anything less than fifteen minutes feels like you've been cheated. You really need to work on your disbelief. Still think I am not a dom?"

"Ugh, God no."

He kissed the inside of her knee.

"Good girl. Lay back, sweet thing, and let me work." She lost track of where his fingers were exactly. Her body pulsed and twitched in places he wasn't even touching. She stopped being able to form whole words and was resorting to grunts and gasps. "Mimi, you still with me?"

"Green."

"I know, sweetheart." She could hear the laughter in his voice and didn't care he was laughing at her. "I'm pretty sure I know the answer but I want to be sure. Are you a virgin?" That stopped her cold. *Was he going to be disappointed that she wasn't?*

"I...don't want to tell you."

"Shit. Are you? I mean I...I didn't think so but I...damn. Okay, maybe we should hold off."

"What?" She was ready to scream. "I'm not; I haven't had tons of lovers but..."

"Oh, thank God. Sorry. I mean, I could work around you being a virgin but it wouldn't be nearly as much fun."

She collapsed back on to the bed in relief. He started teasing her again and her body quickly was back in sync with what he was doing. He rubbed his cheek against her thigh and she jumped. The day-old stubble was actually pretty soft but she was so keyed up and sensitive. On the one hand, he seemed to know all the right places to touch and on the other, he was teasing her so that as soon as she got close, he would switch to something else. She was almost to the point of tears.

"Okay, sweet angel, time to get serious. This is going to be a little different than you are used to but you'll just have to trust me." He wrapped his arm around her legs so they were pinned together. *That couldn't be right?* He bent her knees slightly and she felt him slide his fingers over her labia. *Oh! That felt good.* He teased her for a second and then kissed her hip as he slid two fingers inside her. *Oh dear God, the man had long fingers.* She felt her body pulse deep in her core. She sucked in a breath to try to hold it off and managed to, at least for now.

"Good girl; remember you have to ask permission." She almost growled at him. "Now, there is this bundle of nerves here." She felt his fingers curl slightly and then her eyes rolled back in her head and she let loose a full-throated groan. "Damn, you are so responsive. I love watching you. This gets pretty intense." He stroked inside her again and her body bowed against the restraint at her wrists and where he held her legs. If he did that again, she wouldn't survive and if he didn't do it again, she might kill him. She felt pressure against her clit, not rubbing, like he was pushing a button with his thumb.

"Okay, I'm going to stroke your clit from the inside."

She couldn't have heard him correctly. But then her body seemed to take on a life of its own. She screamed his name, knew there were tears in her eyes but was beyond caring.

"Eric, please! Oh, God. Please!"

"Come for me, angel." She screamed as the light burst behind her eyes. The sounds coming out of her mouth may as well have been a primitive language. Her body convulsed and shook. When she was sure she was going to start coming down, he changed the pressure and the waves continued.

Chapter Five

She was in heaven; that had to be it—she'd died and had been transported. So far, no choirs of angels but she could feel the wings stroking her skin. She frowned just a little. Would you be naked in heaven? May be it was like the Garden of Eden, but paradise was not knowing you were naked and she was starting to be more aware of being naked, not less. The rhythm was constant, a soft silky slap, just fabric against her skin, no pain, and then delicious warmth flowing from her ear down her back to her bottom. If this was death, then maybe it wasn't so bad.

"Welcome back, angel."

"Where did I go?" She couldn't get her eyes to open and if it meant the stroking stopped, she wouldn't open them if you paid her. Something like butterflies tickled her ear and the back of her neck. The stroking now started at her shoulder. She hummed from deep in her chest.

"You tell me." The words bathed her in warmth. *Mmm, so nice.*

"I didn't go anywhere." The angel chuckled in her ear. *Angels don't chuckle.* Maybe they do; she didn't have a lot of experience with angels. She finally managed to peel her eyes open and looked over her shoulder. Not an angel at all, unless you were talking about the fallen kind. More like a sensual pirate.

"I beg to differ; you most definitely went somewhere. How do you feel?"

"Sleepy, like I'm moving through gelatin. Buzzy."

"Your shoulders aren't sore? Nothing pulled?"

"Pulled?"

"How does your, ah, abdomen feel?"

Now she was really starting to feel confused. "Why?"

"Eight? My naughty little angel, I thought you'd say three tops." He was smiling at her. He had such a nice smile, she reached out to trace his lips. She felt drunk on endorphins. *Wait, did he really...?*

"Eric, did you really make me...for eight minutes?"

His smile got wider and his eyebrows spiked up.

"You still owe me one. I didn't want you too freaked out when you came out of subspace."

"Is that what this is called?"

"Mhmm. Some subs find it slightly addictive. I didn't expect you to get there yet, though I should have figured you would."

"Why?"

"Because you are the most receptive, natural sub I have ever met." She snorted and he backed off, and then he moved back to surround her again. "What was the snort for?" His voice sounded hard and even a little mean.

"I mean, look at me." He looked like he was going to yell at her. Not now, not when she was feeling this cherished and protected. "I'm not some tiny little thing. I think my shoulders are wider than yours. I have what my father used to call an old country body. When I would get depressed about the way I looked, he would tell me I was braw and that some highlander would have carried me off to run his fortress and to have his bairns. I was made to wield a sword while a kid was strapped to my hip, not prance around on tiny spikes, simpering and smiling."

He was smiling even more now.

"I could totally see you like that but after you defended hearth and home, you'd curl up and purr in your man's bed."

Her eyes went round.

"I am not a sub." She crossed her arms over her chest and he moved over her, pinning her in place with his body and arms.

"I say you are and at this point I am what, three and oh?"

Damn pirate. She felt his erection against her belly. *Wait...* "Eric, did we, um, did you get off?"

"No. You were barely conscious. Not my idea of fun."

"And now?"

"Mimi, you are still fragile. I'm fine just holding you."

"You can hold me while we have sex." He coughed and choked. "Right now I want you around me, in me, us to join, like nothing I have ever wanted in my life." She flipped him to his back on top of all the pillows and then straddled him. "Does this feel like something a submissive would do? Reach in that drawer and get a condom."

"Mimi, this isn't going to prove anything."

"Just get the condoms."

"Look, you need to know that..."

She shifted over him and pulled the silk kimono out from under her and gasped. She knew she was staring but she couldn't stop. She finally forced herself to blink.

"Oh. My. God. You pierced your..."

"Yeah. I got it to mark my graduation from training. It was supposed to be a mark of my control and it was till I met you and my control went to hell."

She scrambled off of him. He was laid back against the pillows wearing a silk kimono that was too short for him. He was covered in tattoos and now she knew he had a...Prince Albert—the name almost made her giggle. With his long floppy hair, those teal eyes, and the stubble, he looked like a dissolute Englishman in some opium den period drama but the tattoos, earrings, and the piercing were too hard-core for that. No, he was a pirate; a thought went through her like a harp string plucked—her pirate, only hers. Her eyes swept him; thankfully he didn't stop her.

"Can I..." She reached forward and then pulled her hand back.

"I, yeah, I guess. I've had it for years so it is fully healed. I don't even think about it anymore. Unless, of course, a gorgeous woman is looking at me like you are now." She watched as his erection bobbed in the air like it was calling her. Oh hell, maybe it was. She felt an answering pull in her gut. The man made her ache. No man had ever done that: had made her mouth water, made her hungry for him. *Damn skateboarding artist pirate.* She climbed back on the bed.

"Mimi, you're scaring me a little with the look on your face."

"What look?"

"The look that says you are going to eat me alive."

"Oh, you should be afraid, very afraid." She ran her finger lightly over the piercing and watched him gulp down a deep breath. "Does it make it more sensitive?"

"Yeah."

Oh, Mister Chatty was only going to speak in monosyllables now. He was impressive; she had to give him that.

"Condom," she managed to get out. He groaned and handed her a packet. She thought to check the expiration date since she couldn't remember the last time she had had a man in her bedroom. Luckily, while they were close to expired, they weren't quite there yet. She tore the foil open and rolled it down his length. He closed his eyes and gripped the sheets like he was going to die.

She threw a leg over him, trapping his erection between them. She slid forward and the piercing rubbed against her. Even through the latex, she could feel it and threw her head back. As he sat up, she stopped him and slid the kimono off his arms. She wanted to feel him, feel all of her pirate. She moved so that he was notched at her entrance. Before she could think too much, before the uncertainty crept in, she shifted so that he filled her completely.

"Oh. My..."

"God, angel," he breathed in her ear. Her breath caught in her chest and she realized that tears were in her eyes. She swallowed hard as he nuzzled her neck and shoulder. When he realized that she was holding her breath, he flipped them so that she was on her back and eased off her. She wanted to claw at him to bring him back. "Was I hurting you? Are you okay? If it is too much..."

"No, I'm fine. It just caught me by surprise." The hum was back in her chest.

"I can feel you purring." He bent forward and placed kisses down the center of her chest. "You swear I didn't hurt you?"

"I'm fine, Eric. Stop teasing me, dammit."

"Demanding little sub, aren't you." He laughed. She narrowed her eyes and growled at him. Well, she knew a much better use than talking for his mouth. She grabbed the sides of his face, pinning him in place and kissed him hard as he stroked inside her. That felt so good her eyes rolled back in her head. She pulled away to suck air into her lungs and saw his grin. Damn, she wanted to bite the man he was so delicious, and cocky. She would wipe the grin from his face if it broke her. She flipped them again so she was on top. He maneuvered them so he was almost sitting up, too. *Oh damn, that did all the right things.* She felt the first pulse and forced herself to relax and push it away.

"Good girl. You may be on top but I still own your orgasms."

"Oh, I don't think..." He changed his angle and all she could do was groan.

"Don't think, not right now—feel."

All her resistance melted. He had one arm around her hips; with the other hand, he lifted her breast to his lips. He sucked her nipple into his mouth and mimicked the pace set by their hips with his sucking. Her whole body came alive in a way that had never happened before. Then he gently bit down and she gasped as it set off a shockwave that ran through her.

"Not yet, angel. Take a big breath and blow it out." Without even thinking about it, she did as he said and the tension building in her body became manageable again.

"Good. I'm going to do that again." As he started the process again, her body knew what to expect this time and started to anticipate it.

"Oh, Eric." Her voice sounded pleading and soft.

"Mmm, baby, you want this, don't you?" She nodded and curled into his shoulder since her head had become too heavy to hold up anymore. She felt drugged and hyper-aware at the same time. "When you look at me like that, I can't refuse you. Come for me, baby." He rocked forward again and she opened her mouth in a soundless scream. As he held her, she felt his own orgasm start. She wrapped him tightly in her arms, suddenly feeling very protective of him.

They lay collapsed on the bed, twined around one another, panting for several minutes.

"Angel, you are going to ruin me."

She'd have laughed if she could catch her breath. She traced out a design on his stomach and then bent her head to kiss it. She needed sleep but she hadn't eaten since breakfast and she guessed neither had he. She forced herself to move and stretch.

"I'm starved." She saw his smirk and pulled a pillow over his face. "I haven't eaten since breakfast and I'll bet you haven't either. I make a hell of a grilled cheese, that is, if you eat cheese? The soup was just vegetables and some olive oil." He put his hand on her thigh and all her senses focused on that one spot.

"Grilled cheese actually sounds delicious right now."

She got up and all her anxieties about her body came roaring back. She ducked into her closet and pulled on yoga pants and a XXXL men's shirt that came to mid-thigh on her.

In the kitchen, she quickly put together the sandwiches and put them in the hot pan. Eric came out in the silk kimono Audi had brought back from Japan for her. He'd left it untied and she kept sneaking peeks at his body. He was all long, lean lines that made her tongue itch to lick up and down them. Her inner elephant was wearing a housedress and curlers. He came up behind her and wrapped her in his arms. She pushed all her anxiety aside and let the sensations overtake her. His lips were on her neck; his teeth gently scraped the spot behind her ear that made her shiver. His hand dropped to undo some of the buttons on her shirt and he reached in to caress her breast. She hung suspended in his arms, glazed with want.

"You make me hungry for more than just food." He kissed her jaw. "But I better let you cook or someone is going to get hurt."

***

She promised herself she wasn't going to look but she knew she was lying. She craned her neck to look at her front porch and sure enough there he was. Her heart did a backflip and the rest of her got all hot and wet. It had been three weeks and every day she expected him to beg off, to come up with an excuse that would signal the beginning of the end. So far, not even a hint he was getting bored, or that he was tired of dealing with her insecurities. If anything, she was the one getting fed up with her behavior and had decided he was at least getting a key tonight and if it worked out then maybe he could move in. It would be weird when Audi was around but they would have to find a way to work it out.

She walked up the steps with a big grin on her face. It had pretty much taken up permanent residence there and she didn't see it leaving any time soon.

"Hey, gorgeous." He gave her a big kiss and wrapped her in his arms. Oh, this was so where she wanted to be. She got lost in kissing him back. Damn, her heart was pounding in her chest. "So, interesting choice of music for Rose." She cocked her head and heard growling guitars and screaming lyrics. She hadn't left one of her sister's CDs on. *Oh no. Oh hell no, not now. Please not now.*

"Um, how 'bout we go out to dinner? My treat! You can pick the place," she almost yelled.

"Fine, but I've gotten kinda used to walking Rose and holding my girl's hand. So we can go after." He held her hand to his lips. When had her dominant pirate turned so cute and mushy? She groaned; there was no avoiding this. They had to meet sometime. She wriggled out of his grasp and tried to put her key in the lock. Maybe if she could sneak in and talk to Audi first? He draped himself around her and took the key from her fumbling hands, unlocking the door and pushing it open before steering her in.

Audi walked out in an old beat-up black T-shirt, ripped up fishnets under cut-off jean shorts that were cut shorter than anything Mimi would ever wear. The outfit was finished off with shiny combat boots. Her face was obscured by the take-out carton she was shoveling food into her mouth from. All you could see was her two-tone black and platinum crop.

"Mim, there isn't even any chicken in the fridge. Don't tell me you've suddenly turned into a veg-head on me?"

She felt Eric's whole body go stiff behind her. She sucked in what little air she could with the herd of elephants sitting on her lungs at the moment.

"Aud, I'd like to introduce you to my..." She blanked. What were they? Friends with serious benefits? Boyfriend sounded ridiculous. Lover? She'd love to introduce him like that; at least that felt true.

"I'm the guy who loves your sister. Eric Tolland." Mimi saw Audi's head snap up when Eric spoke. She supposed she would react the same way if some guy walked into the living room and...Wait! He'd announced he loved her. He must have just panicked. That had to be it because no rational man just said "Hi, I love your sister," like it was no big deal.

"Rik?"

"Um, no, Eric. Mimi, why don't you take Rose for a quick walk and then we can go get some dinner? I'll stay here and tell your sister all about me since she looks ready to grill me, anyway."

Mimi looked over at Audi and she did not look happy one bit.

"Maybe I should stay here."

Audi piped up. "I promise there will still be pieces of him left when you get back. Go. I promise not to hurt him. Hey, I'm the big sister, remember?"

Mimi looked at her five-foot-two sister and scoffed. She hadn't been the '"big" sister since they were in elementary school. She didn't know what was going on here but she didn't like it one bit.

"So Rawdy Maudi... I'm an idiot. Mimi said she had an in at the recording studio. Was going to hook me up with tickets and backstage passes.

I almost burst out laughing and told her I had
sponsored the Harridans' last tour."

"Rik Toil, you wanna explain what the hell
you are doing with my little sister?"

"Your little sister is a grown woman of
twenty-nine. I am not doing anything she
doesn't want me to do."

"Why the false identity?"

"Actually, Rik Toil is the fake ID. I really am
Eric Tolland. Look, your sister doesn't know
anything about that life and at least for now I'd
like it to stay that way."

"Afraid she'll take your money?"

"No, dammit. Just the opposite—she'll run
screaming for the hills. Maudi, I wasn't kidding
when I said I love her. I just wanted the chance
to have her know me, Eric Tolland, before she
has to deal with all the bullshit of Rik Toil."

"Rik, if you hurt her, I'll slice you to ribbons."

"No doubt. So you won't tell her?"

"I'm home till Tuesday. You've got till
Monday to tell her the truth."

"Shit. Fine, but I really feel like it is too early.
I mean, we've only been together three weeks
and well, it's not like she is yelling she loves me
from the rooftop, even if I feel that way about

her." He looked at his feet and felt more than a little hopeless. Audi started laughing.

"You really do care about her, don't you? I mean, every time I have ever seen you you've got a girl on each arm and are smiling for some camera, playing the cool customer. This is a whole new side of you. My sister is one of the nicest, most understanding people I know and when she makes her mind up about someone, she is loyal to a fault. If you really do love her, you need to trust her with this."

The front door opened and Mimi rushed in, breathless.

"Okay, I don't see any blood on the floor, so that is a good sign."

"Your sister told me that if I hurt you she'll slice me to ribbons."

Mimi made a face at Maude.

"Sounds like her. Are you ready to go out for some dinner?"

"Change in plans. I'm treating both of you, that is, if your sister can stand going to a restaurant that serves veg-head food."

"Eric, I'd rather you saved your money and..."

"Not listening. Don't make me get persuasive, angel." Just calling Mimi "angel" set something off in her and she melted a little before his very eyes. Shit, he had to come up with a way to do this and not screw it up. He'd never wanted anything more in his life.

Maude chimed in. "That's okay, you two go out. I'm kind of beat, anyway. The tour is on the verge of collapsing because our manager couldn't handle the finances so I'm ending up with his job and mine. I finally fired him. I just want to sleep for the next three days. Just bring me home some leftovers and I'm good."

"Audi, you sure?'"

"Yeah, besides I don't know if I could stand watching you two mooning at each other, knowing the only guys I'm going to see are roadies and drunken fans for the next six months."

Mimi leaned over and gave her sister a hug.

"We'll talk when I get back. Go get some sleep; you do look exhausted."

***

He watched her creep back in the bedroom. "How's your sister?"

"Completely out of it. I worry about her, especially now that she's had to fire their tour manager. She can't do the business stuff all day and then sing all night."

"She looks like a tough cookie; I'm sure she'll be fine." He made a mental note to talk to Steve about finding someone to help Audi out. "If I were you, I'd worry more about myself, my naughty angel." He watched her eyes get wide.

"I...Wha...Oh hell."

He laughed at her.

"A friend in the studio? You'd see what you could do to get me some tickets? Why were you so evasive?"

"Guys get a little stupid when they find out who she is. Either they think I'm like her, which obviously I'm not, or they decide why drive the sedan when you can have the racecar. I just wanted one relationship that it wasn't on the table. I didn't mean to lie, exactly."

"What should your punishment be?"

"Punishment!" she stage whispered.

"Mmm, definitely. I think a ten-minute orgasm."

"That doesn't sound like punishment."

"If you can't make a sound, it will be. Wouldn't want to wake your sister up, now would you? Left to your own reactions, you can get kinda loud." That was one of the things he loved about her. She made love with abandon, nothing held back. He knew he should check the smirk on his face but she was already getting that glazed look in her eyes and he could see her squeezing her thighs together, trying to assuage the ache. But it was the little shiver thing she did that was the biggest turn-on. That was his favorite part.

***

Mimi swallowed hard and pushed the glass revolving door open. *She could do this!* Audi had put the idea in her head. If it backfired, she was losing her job but...for some weird reason she didn't think it would. She shifted her portfolio to her other hand and hit the elevator button. She really wanted a shot of courage right about now and fished her phone out of her purse. The elevator was taking forever anyway. She hit his name and heard it ring.

"Hey, beautiful!"

She smiled; she felt better already.

"Hey to you, too, handsome. Do you have a couple of minutes?"

"For you, the rest of my life."

He'd spent the weekend saying stuff like that and every time he did, her stomach did the thing where she felt like she was on a carnival ride, excited and terrified at the same time. Crap, if she lost her job then they would both have crappy jobs and she really wanted to show his portfolio to some of the other art directors. He just needed to put himself out there; he was too good not to.

"I need some courage."

"Sure, what are you going to do?"

"Remember the account I was crying about when we met?"

"Honestly, I was only thinking about the gorgeous woman in my arms at the time. So I have the vaguest memory. Something about you being excluded from some meeting?"

"Yes, sorta. I was telling Audi about it and she suggested that I talk to the head guy and show him what I've done. If it works, I may end up with an account of my own; if it doesn't, I could end up looking for a new job."

"Hey, don't worry about it. I've got some cash set aside; I could help you out."

"I don't think so, mister. You'll need it if something happens and you get hurt. I really want you to let me show your portfolio around, too. You're too good to not be working or at least in a gallery. Those sketches you did of me while I was hoop dancing were amazing."

"I was inspired. You inspire me."

"I can still inspire you and you can make a living with your art. Hang on a sec. I need to talk to the receptionist." She pressed the phone to her hip while she got directions. *Okay, that was a lot easier than she anticipated.* They had a pretty laid back place here.

"Hey, still there?"

"Still here. Where do you want to go tonight?"

"If he throws me out, I'm curling up in bed and not coming out."

"Nah, no man is going to throw you out. Trip over his tongue maybe, but not toss you."

"Okay, I'm here. Wish me luck."

"You'll do great. I love you."

Tears backed up in her eyes and she swallowed to clear the knot in her throat.

"Love you, too." She heard his breath catch on the other end but she meant it. What ever happened, she was here for the long haul.

She knocked on the door as Eric said he had to go. The voice on the other side of the door said to come in. When she entered, she was staring at the back of a chair and a view of Pike Place that belonged on postcards. Then the chair swiveled and she gasped.

"Eric! What are you doing here? Oh, shit! Come on, you shouldn't be there."

"Mimi! I..."

The door swung open and Steve walked in. "Rik, can I get you to look over these projections? I wanted to go over some changes I think we should make to..." He looked up from the stack of papers in his hands. "Oh, hey Cinderella. You taking him to lunch?" He looked back and forth between the two of them and backed toward the door. "Um, this stuff can wait. I'll talk to you later," he mumbled.

"Mimi, I can explain."

"You are supposed to be here? He called you Rik. You're Rik Toil." The pieces were starting to fall together. "Did you have fun laughing about the stupid girl that didn't know who you were? All the times I told you that you could make money with your art. Did you go home and crack up at how gullible I was? Was there anything you didn't lie to me about?"

"Mimi, angel—"

"Don't you dare! Oh, my God. Was this just sport for you? Fuck with the big girl for fun? See what you could get her to do? Go after the big girl; no one asks them to dance, they show their appreciation so much more!" Tears were streaming down her face now and she tried to scrape them from her cheeks. Eric had come around to her side of the desk. "Don't you dare touch me!" If she didn't get out of there now, she was going to break down and completely lose it. He reached for her and she threw her portfolio in front of her to block his touch. When she moved toward the door, he blocked her escape. "Eric, let me go!" Her voice had turned into a wail.

"Mimi, I was going to tell you, I swear. I was going to do it tonight. I never meant for it to end up like this. I love you."

"People that love each other don't lie to each other. Get out of my way, Eric, or I swear I will..."

He stepped aside and in the corner of her mind that was still rational, she noted how sad he looked when he did it. Unfortunately, the rest of her was too hurt and pissed off to care. She had already taken the day off work so she had nowhere to go but home. First, she stopped at the store and loaded her basket with all the junk food she had ever dreamed about. When she got home, she slammed the door so hard a picture fell off the wall. She glared at it but left it there.

Audi stuck her head out of her room. "What the hell, Mim?"

She broke down and slid to her knees, sobbing. Audi had her arms around her before she hit the ground.

"Sweetheart? Mimi? What happened? Tell me what happened."

It was minutes before she could get her sobbing under control enough to make sense.

"He lied. Making fun of me. Audi!" *God, it hurt so bad.* Her heart was breaking.

"Mimi, you mean Eric?" She nodded furiously as a fresh set of sobbing rocked her. "Dammit! I told him to tell you."

Mimi pulled out of her sister's arms.

"You knew! You knew and you didn't say anything!" Audi tried to put her arms around her again but Mimi threw them off. Lied to by Eric was bad enough but betrayed by her sister stung even worse. "Don't touch me!"

She grabbed her stuff and ran to her room, locking the door behind her. Her phone started ringing and she looked to see who it was. Eric's face flashed on the screen. She hit Ignore. Two minutes later, the phone rang again and she hit Ignore and turned it off. She got into her oldest, most comfortable sweats and started opening the bags of junk food. She ignored the scraping at the door. Audi the traitor could take Rose out. She had sampled some of everything and was going back for seconds when her door fell in to the room.

Audi stood there, tossing a screwdriver in the air.

"You didn't really think a little thing like a locked door was going to keep me out, did you? You forget I'm much more devious than you. Oh hell, what are you eating? Are those the disgusting circus peanuts you like? Something marshmallow that tastes like banana should not be orange. Give me all that stuff—you'll just end up making yourself sick along with miserable." She started throwing all the junk back into the bag till she got to the chocolate covered peppermint cremes. "Oh! God, I love these!" She started unwrapping one, popped it into her mouth and plopped herself down on the bed.

Mimi looked at her sister and heaved a sigh. She couldn't really hate her. The damn pixie was

frustrating but even when they were girls, all
Audi had to do was make a funny face and she
would crack up, all her anger forgotten.

"Since when did you become the junk food
police?"

"Since I realized living on this stuff was
doing nothing for my performances. I'm not
about to stop eating a burger now and then but
yeah, we have fruit baskets backstage and real
meals with vegetables and everything. That was
one of the reasons I had to shit can Herve. He
wasn't taking care of the details and our
performances were suffering." She popped
another candy in her mouth. "Mmm, still love
these, though."

"Audi, when did you know?"

"Friday, when you guys walked in. Rik Toil
Boards was one of the sponsors of our last tour.
I'd met him a bunch backstage. Mim, he was
different with you. I don't think he was playing
you. Not really. He said he wanted the chance to
tell you himself; that is the only reason I didn't
say anything. He had till tonight to come clean."
Mimi felt tears sliding down her cheeks again
and leaned into her sister as Audi tucked an arm
around her shoulders.

"Audi, I think my heart is broken."

"I know, honey. You'll get through this. Quit your job and come on tour with me."

"I can't do that."

"I know; I was just being selfish. I'd love to have you there. I spend my nights singing about sex and love and rock n' roll and I'm only getting one out of the three. I'm a damn rock star. It is pathetic." Audi started laughing and Mimi couldn't help but join her. Audi didn't do self-pity and didn't let anyone around her indulge, either. "Um, I gotta ask. Word was Rik, I mean Eric, was into some, ah... He didn't do anything I have to have some of the roadies kill him for, did he?"

"No! He's not like any guy I've ever...well, not that there were lots of them but...God, the sex was amazing. Even before I was sure I was in love with him. Oh, Audi..." Mimi hid her face against the bed and her sister rubbed her back.

"Okay, just to let you know—you got all the wrong stuff to get over a breakup. You need either hard liquor or soft ice cream and really bad movies. Come on, I'm popping popcorn." Audi pulled on her arm and Mimi followed her against her will.

A Heath Ledger marathon ending with *10 Things I Hate About You* later, she still felt like crap but she'd be able to leave the house tomorrow. She turned her phone on and it rang immediately, scaring the hell out of her. It was still Eric. She hit Ignore and checked to see if anyone else had called. Nope, but there were twenty-five messages from him. She selected them all and erased them. She considered taking his info out of her contact list but then she'd never recognize his number. She just moved him out of favorites and went to delete his picture. Instead, she just ran her fingers over it like she would have liked to in real life. She snapped the phone off instead and crawled into bed. She lay awake for hours, looking at all the drawings he'd done of her. No one that could look at her and see that kind of beauty should have been able to lie to her the way he did. She got up and walked to where one was taped to the wall. They were too nice to destroy but looking at them now hurt too much. She started pulling them down and put them in her flat file.

Chapter Six

"Evie?"

"Eric? Are you alright? You sound like hell."

"She won't talk to me. My angel won't talk to me."

"Are you drunk?"

"Yeah."

"You never drink. Are you home? I don't know what I can do on the opposite coast but maybe I can call you a cab or something?"

"I'm home, alone. I really fucked up, Evie."

"It can't be that bad."

"I didn't tell her the truth; my angel deserved the truth. She could have handled the truth."

"What are we talking about here, little brother?"

"I just wanted her to love me, stupid Eric, not that damn Rik Toil. God, I hate him."

"And she would rather have Rik Toil?"

"No! She loved me; she said so. But then she found out about him and it all went to hell."

"So get rid of him. He's not real. He's a caricature you created. Turn him into a cartoon or a logo or whatever and be done with him. Companies rebrand themselves all the time. Do it and then take some time off. Come play uncle for a little while. The kids miss you. Figure out what you want to do next. Get back into your art."

Eric moaned.

"I can't do that, either. She was my muse. Evie, she was perfect, at least to me. I don't think she ever really believed me, though."

"Oh, baby brother, I'm sorry. I know I didn't believe Joseph the first hundred or so times he said it, either. You just have to get her to believe it."

"What worked with you?"

"Sheer relentlessness. Thank God my husband is stubborn as hell. It's okay, though; his daughter is just like him so I'm getting even in a big way."

"You are evil."

"That is me, Evil Evie. So if it works out, you gonna marry her?"

"If she'll let me."

"Don't give her the option. Just tell her she's marrying you and be done with it. Mom will have the whole thing planned in a second for you."

"I think Mimi would want to plan her own wedding."

"Mimi, huh? I like it. Sober up and wow her, little brother. When you turn on the Tolland charm, you can be irresistible. All you Tolland men are. You are the only one who didn't believe it."

***

Thursday, the wall of scent hit her as soon as she stepped off the elevator. *Did someone die?* The other elevator door opened and Sharon stepped out. Mimi let out a sigh and walked into the reception area with Sharon hot on her heels. There were vases of flowers everywhere. There was every kind of flower she could imagine and some she couldn't. She wanted to talk to as few people as possible today with as fragile as she felt, so she ducked her head and started toward the back.

"Oh, thank God, you're finally here."

She heard Sharon stop and turn toward Megan, the receptionist. "All these are for me?"

Mimi smirked; she could only imagine what Sharon had to do to deserve a floral delivery on this level. She was almost through reception when she saw Megan shake her head and point at her.

"No, they are for Mimi."

"Her?" Sharon almost screeched.

"Me?"

Megan nodded her head yes.

"Who could have sent you all these?" Sharon grabbed a card from one of the vases and opened it.

"What does this mean?" She held out the card like it was radioactive. The only thing written on it was "Talk to me, please'."

"I think it means someone wants me to talk to them." She started plucking all the cards from the other bouquets. She hoped Eric didn't write anything too personal in the cards but she wasn't taking any chances.

"But who could want...Wait! Is this the loser from the bar a couple of weeks ago?"

Mimi felt herself go pale with anger. Anger was good; she wouldn't break down in tears if she was ticked off.

"What, in your opinion, exactly made him a loser? That he wasn't in a suit, his hair was too long, he saw through your bullshit instantly, or was it just he chose me over you?" Out of the corner of Mimi's eye, she saw Megan silently clapping. *Guess Sharon didn't just get to her.* Okay, now that Mimi the Destroyer was out of the bag, she was not going away easily.

"Megan, are any of the partners in this morning?"

"Um, yeah, all of them. Something is going on with one of the big accounts. You want an appointment?"

"Yes, please. If I'm going to be kicking ass, I may as well start with the real problem and then this penny-ante crap won't tick me off as much." She cocked her thumb at Sharon. The woman was pale and looked like she was going to cry.

"Sharon, you deserved every bit of that for the way you treat the other women around here but you aren't the real problem. The macho bullshit ends today. Either you are with me or you aren't."

Megan's eyes couldn't get wider and stay in her head. Sharon just gave a small shake of her head no.

Megan put the phone down. "Um, it seems they were about to call you. Mimi, are you sure you want to do this? I mean, now?"

Oh, hell she was probably out of a job already; they may as well know what was going on behind their backs.

She dumped her bag in the drawer and started opening the note cards to see if Eric had left any clues as to whether he had gotten her fired. As upset as she was, she didn't think he was the type. *Oh crap!* Her ideas for the Rik Toil campaign. Well, now she was actually glad the guys had cut her out. Most of the notes just said "talk to 'me" in one form or another. A few were sketches she recognized as her. Just little things that made her cry with wanting him. She called Megan and had her send the flowers to the children's hospital to get handed out.

She ducked into the bathroom to pull herself together. She stared into the mirror for a minute and took a few deep breaths. She heard someone sniffling in one of the stalls.

"Sharon?"

"What? Got more things you want to say to me?" Suddenly, the stall door banged open and Sharon slammed out of it. "You know, I do the best I can with what I've got. I was never the talented one; I wasn't the smart one. All I ever heard was that I was cute or pretty or whatever. So I did the pageant stuff because that was what I was good at and then I ended up in sales because guys liked to buy things from me. I'm a damn good account manager but does anyone give me credit? No, so I play it up for the boys and you all hate me for it."

"God, this is high school all over again. Tell you what, I'll start taking more notice of what you are doing with the accounts and you quit making me feel like a dancing elephant."

"I never said you were a dancing elephant. Even I'm not that bitchy."

"You're right, actually; I said it. Truce?" Mimi stuck her hand out. Sharon looked at it for a second and then spit in hers.

"High school, right?"

Mimi smiled, spit in her hand and shook. "High school. Only, we are totally taking this place back from the stupid frat boys. Okay, can I wash my hand now? 'Cause that was kinda gross then and now, well, ick."

"Totally!" They both cracked up and dashed for the sinks. It was the first time Mimi could remember Sharon really laughing and not some stupid giggle meant to catch some guy's ear.

"Okay, I'm off to get fired now."

"Crap. You really think so?"

"Why else would all three partners want to talk to me?"

"Promotion?" Her voice didn't exactly sell it.

"Yeah, right and then they are giving me the keys to the company car."

"We have a company car? Wait. That was a blonde moment, wasn't it?"

"You said it; I didn't. Gotta go."

Sharon held up her hands with her fingers crossed.

She ran her hands over her skirt and took a deep breath. As she knocked on the door, she put a pleasant smile on her face she really didn't feel.

"Come in."

Mimi walked in to see the three partners sitting in club chairs, Gerry standing near one of them, and Eric sitting on the couch. Her eyes swept his expensive Italian shoes and a suit that cost more than her couch; his hair was slicked back and looked darker now. He had on blue wrap-around sunglasses like Bono wore. The guy sitting there bore almost no resemblance to her pirate-artist but her body knew it was him.

"Ms. Ferguson, have a seat." Mr. Comstock motioned toward the couch. Eric just smiled like a cat right before it devours the defenseless bird. She walked over to the couch without looking at him again. Her damn body was buzzing and she couldn't think. She sat like she was made of wood.

"Coffee, Ms. Ferguson?" Eric asked her.

"No, thank you." She answered without looking at him or even turning toward him.

"Cookies? They're quite good."

She almost started laughing but then remembered he'd lied to her.

"It is nine o'clock in the morning. No. Thanks." She had to bite the inside of her cheek to keep from smiling. Doing this in front of her bosses made it feel sexy-naughty; combined with the sexual charge she felt coming off him, it was all she could do not to run screaming from the room. "You wanted to see me, sirs?"

Comstock looked at the other partners and then started. "Ms. Ferguson, Mimi, it has come to our attention that you are solely responsible for the ideas here for the Rik Toil account." Gerry caught her eye and smiled at her. Okay, maybe she *wasn't* getting fired.

"Yes, sir."

"Was there a reason that you didn't present them at the roundtable?"

"I was advised they would, um, hold more water, if they were presented by someone who..." She swallowed hard. "That looked more like a skateboarder, sir."

"I see. We evidently have a few men that could use some sensitivity training."

"Or a damn whipping." Comstock turned and glared at Mitchell.

"George, you are going to get us sued." He shook his head. The rest either cracked up or nodded their heads, including her damn pirate.

"Yes, well, whipping aside. You will have complete control of the Rik Toil account and it is about to get much larger. Why don't you explain, Mr. Toil, er, I mean Tolland. Sorry, still getting used to the change."

"No need to apologize. I expect it will take everyone a while to get used to it. Ms. Ferguson, as you may have guessed, I have decided that it is time to put Rik Toil away, at least on a personal level. Rik Toil Boards will continue but I think it is time to rebrand."

"Why me?"

"I plan to work closely with whoever takes this on. When I found out that you had done the work for the campaign, I was impressed. As Rik Toil, I always demanded the best. I don't see a reason for that to stop now when I am working under my real name." He leaned toward her and her body leaned toward him, even as she was telling it to move away. He hadn't said anything the least bit flirtatious but her stomach hopped on the carnival ride anyway. "And Mimi," she realized she was holding her breath, "you are the best." His voice was almost a whisper. It felt like a caress. She gasped but he was the only one who noticed. The corners of his mouth kicked up just the tiniest bit and she could see the crinkles at the corners of his eyes deepen.

"Yes, she is, Eric," Mr. Comstock said. "Now, would you want her to work on the foundation branding also?"

"Foundation?" She finally looked him in the eye.

"Yes, I've had some things happen in my personal life that have made me think more about how to give back. I am in a unique position; the kids trust me because of my street cred. I want to start out with funding some after-school arts and sports programs in schools that need them with the idea that we can package programs schools can pick and choose from and move them around to more schools. I don't want it to feel like some sad poverty program, though, so I want a full promo schedule, logos everywhere, T-shirts, boards, celeb endorsements, the works. Anything we sell will offset the cost of the programs. Schools can bring it in on a sliding scale based on the incomes of the neighborhood."

She couldn't help it; she smiled then and he looked at her like she had given him something better than diamonds. She ducked her head.

"I want Sharon to work on the endorsements. Send her down to LA. She can talk anyone into anything, especially if they're guys."

"If you feel that would be best," Comstock interjected.

"Sharon, the perky blonde? Hell, I'd buy whatever she was selling," Mitchell said to no one in particular.

"George, someone is going to get whipped if he doesn't keep his mouth shut. Ignore him, Mimi; we do."

She held off the urge to giggle. Mitchell was more than a little disinhibited.

"How will the branding be tied to Rik Toil Boards?"

"It won't. I'm going to be taking a sabbatical to start the foundation but other than a founding sponsor, there won't be any crossover."

She looked at him hard. *He was stepping down from his company?*

"Eric, is this a good idea when you are rebranding? People are cynical and they'll assume there is something you are trying to hide."

"I'll tell anyone and everyone. I fell in love and the woman wouldn't have me."

Her eyes went wide. He was saying all of this in front of her bosses. Part of her was thrilled at the words, well, at least the fell in love part. The rest of this was just manipulative. He wanted her to develop a brand for the foundation from scratch, rebrand his company and all so she would be forced to work with him. "I plan to take some time off, hang out with my sisters, see my folks, play with my niece and nephew. When I get back, I want to see what you've got and we can start work from there. What do you say?"

She couldn't believe she was going to do this. Four days ago, this man had been her lover. Her body swayed but she caught herself. Working with him would be torture even if it was the chance of a lifetime.

"I quit." The words were out of her mouth and she gasped. She thought about taking them back but that didn't feel right either.

"You what?" Comstock choked.

"I quit. I'll give you two weeks' notice."

"Can I ask why?"

"I...I'm going to manage my sister's tour." She hoped to hell Audi hadn't found anyone yet.

"I see. When were you planning on telling us?" She ducked her head. "Yes, well, I suppose that changes things. Mr. Tolland, I'm sure we can find a suitable replacement for Ms. Ferguson..."

"No, if Mimi can't do it, I don't want someone else to handle it. I..." He looked at her and she thought he might crumble. He looked so defeated, her heart ached. She couldn't believe he wasn't going to go through with it. They were such good ideas. The foundation, the rebranding so he could get his life back. She had hurt him in a way his lying to her hadn't hurt her. She stood to leave and the men all stood too, except Eric, who looked like he couldn't quite remember how.

She made it back to her cubicle. She hated the stupid open plan office. She just wanted somewhere she could hide. She buried her head in her arms on her desk. From the tap of the heels, she knew Sharon had walked up.

"You okay?"

"No," she said without lifting her head.

"Anything I can do?"

"No, thanks."

"How 'bout me?" a male voice said. Her head snapped up.

"Eric."

"Aren't you Rik Toil?" Mimi could feel Sharon start to turn on the charm, like it was a reflex reaction she had no control over. She hadn't really expected the woman to change in the course of an hour.

"Sharon, if you value your hands in any way you will keep them off him. Do I make myself exceedingly clear?"

The woman's eyes went wide.

"Wait, your los...er, guy is 'freakin' Rik Toil? Damn, girl!"

"He's not mine."

"Yes, I am, but you won't listen to me."

"Eric, I am not doing this here. I really didn't appreciate you manipulating me in there."

"I got that when you rather quit than work on the project."

"You quit!" Sharon screeched.

Great! Now the entire office knew. Hell, it saved her having to write a memo.

"Yes. I need to call my sister. Can I get some privacy?"

"Sure." Sharon immediately left. She stared pointedly at Eric.

"Go ahead and call Audi. I'm not leaving till we talk."

"Eric, we have talked."

"Maybe, but you haven't listened, my stubborn angel."

"Don't. I am not your angel. Eric, I went through all the press clippings; I saw all the girls you date. I saw the type and man, do you have a type. Half dressed, tight bodied, blonde, lots of eyeliner, lots of tattoos, lots of piercings. I can't ever really compete, can I? You think you want me but it really is just that I'm different for now. And when you get bored, you'll revert to type."

"So there is nothing I can say or do. That is just it. Judge. Jury. Executioner."

Tears welled in her eyes. *Shit, this hurt.*

"Don't make it worse; we had a good three weeks."

"Is that all I was? A good three weeks? Let you play on the wild side a little and now you're done? God, and to think I fell in love with your softness. Soft skin, soft heart, the kind of heart that would spend the time to coax a scared dog out of her trauma. The kind that might see me as something other than what everyone else does. I've never been so sorry to be wrong." He stood up and moved away from her desk.

She felt like she couldn't breathe.

She could call Audi from somewhere else. She couldn't be here another second. She grabbed her bag and ran into the stairwell. The first sob hit her just past the door. She felt like she was going to be sick and sat in the middle of the stairs, doubled over.

Chapter Seven

"Uncle Rik?"

"Yeah, buddy?"

"You're not as much fun as you used to be."
He looked down at the little boy with his sister's
eyes and his brother-in-law's black curls.

"Sorry, girl problems."

"Girls are yucky. Marie at school is always
trying to kiss me."

"Do you let her?"

"No. I chase Maggie."

Eric shook his head. The kid was in
preschool.

"So do you kiss her?"

"Sometimes, but she runs fast so she is hard
to catch."

"My girl is hard to catch, too."

"When I want to catch Maggie, I let Marie
catch me and then Maggie has a fight with her
and the winner gets to kiss me."

"Does your mother know all this is going on?" The kid stood stock-still. "Your secret is safe with me, but fair warning—one of these days they are going to turn on you and you better be able to outrun both of them."

Actually, the kid may have the right idea. What is the phrase—out of the mouths of babes? He flicked on his phone.

"Steve?"

"If it isn't the prodigal boss. Finally bored? Coming back soon? Please? Seriously, I'm dying here."

"Sorry, no. Not yet. I'm still working on how to get Mimi back."

"Still stuck on Cinderella? Look man, I think after eight weeks you have your answer."

"I can't give up. I mean, if I thought she didn't love me or she was toxic but she's not, she's just scared and I have to find a way to get past the walls she's got up. She let me in once and I blew it. I won't make the same mistake again. Listen, I think I've been going about this all wrong. I want you to get in touch with the tour company and offer to sponsor the rest of the 'Harridans' tour."

"Sure, we got a lot of bounce when we did it last time. But, what does this have to do with Cinderella?"

"She's the touring manager right now. Her sister is with the band and she is pitching in."

"Want me to check on their financials? I mean, if we are going to be sponsors we have the right."

"No more than you usually do. I'm sure Mimi is running a tight ship. Mostly I just want an excuse to be in her face every night. Giving her space hasn't exactly worked so I'm going to crowd her a little."

"I know you; you don't ever do anything a little. Give me an hour and I'll get back to you with the details. Any special concessions you want? Hourly meetings with the tour manager, maybe? I'm assuming you'll be on site a lot."

"I'm moving in with them. I'm running away and taking the circus with me. I want the whole show. The semi with the ramps we pull out for the X Games; I want part of the team at every stop. I want a 'freakin' event every time we pull into town. Pre-press, posters, team signings, the works."

"All this to get a girl?"

"No, it makes good business sense, too. It will build some buzz so when the rebranding happens we've got our asses covered."

"Sold me. Okay, let me get to work. I'll call you as stuff starts happening. Where are they playing right now?"

"Conveniently enough, they're over in Worcester tonight. I may take a run over and check out one of my favorite bands."

"Un huh. You know, I am really am glad we're friends and not enemies."

"Make this happen and you'll be my best friend."

"Asshole. Talk to you soon."

He'd forgotten about dinner with his parents. He'd definitely lucked out with them. Although Evie's kids satisfied some of his mother's crazy grandmother cravings, he could feel her looking at him, thinking he was next, wondering when he was going to show up with a girl and make the big announcement. Well, if this worked out she wouldn't have to wait too much longer.

At least he'd gotten there in time for the encore. The energy from the crowd was amazing. You could feel it pulse in waves, even hidden backstage where he was. Audi was the last one off stage and looked at him like he was a ghost.

"What are you doing here?"

"We're your new tour sponsor, or will be by tomorrow."

She nodded her head, shaking all the earrings and the bits of metal woven into her hair.

"This wouldn't have anything to do with my sister, would it?"

"Nah." He nodded his head yes, and then smiled. "It's all good business. We are going to bring in the whole circus starting with the next venue—Hartford, right?"

"Yeah, so the ramps and the team? All of it?"

"All of it."

"And you are going to need to stick close to watch over your investment, of course?"

"Of course. Where is she?"

"Where she is every night. Come on, I'll take you but then I have to talk to the band for a while. Can I trust you?"

"What do you think?"

"No. But she's been miserable for the last two months so maybe this isn't as stupid as it seems."

"Your sister redefines stubborn."

"Preaching to the choir. I had to share a room with her for years—you have no idea."

"No, but I'd like to."

She just laughed at him.

"Come on, lover boy."

He actually had butterflies at the thought of seeing Mimi again. He cleared his head. He loved her, she loved him; she had said it and he didn't think it was something she said easily. He wasn't happy at the thought of her miserable, although it was her own damn fault. His stubborn angel. When they got this behind them, he was going to sit her down and have a serious talk about who was in charge here. He followed Audi through the tunnels till they came up at the back of the house. Soon they were in the control room for the lights and sound systems. As they arrived, the last of the techs was leaving. Audi held her finger to her lips and pushed the door open quietly.

"She is so not one of the party people. Every night I come up here and wake her up to go back to our bus." He looked down at the couch and wanted to laugh. There was his sweet angel, curled up on a loveseat that was way too small for her to actually sleep on but she was completely crashed. She even had her hands tucked under her chin. His heart ached all over again.

"Should we get her up?" he whispered.

"No. If you can carry her, bring her down to the bus. She works herself ragged and doesn't eat. I'm worried about her."

"Um, mind if I stay with her? I mean, I don't like the idea of her being there alone."

"Yeah, right, that's it. You don't fool me. You look like hell, too. God, I really don't want a front row seat to the two of you making up but I suppose I'm stuck with you both for the duration."

He grinned from ear to ear and kissed Audi on the top of her head.

"I promise to take really good care of her."

"You better or you're dead."

He bent and slid his arms under Mimi. It was as if his whole body sighed with relief when he held her. He managed to get a roadie to lead him to the girls' bus and get her into bed. He seriously considered undressing her but figured she would tear him apart if he did. That didn't mean she wasn't going to wake up in his arms, though.

***

Mmm. She felt like she finally slept. She was having the best dream—so real, she could smell her pirate's scent, spicy and exotic. She had buried her face in his chest and inhaled as her body calmed. She could feel his skin against her lips, smooth and warm. God, he was always so warm; she loved that. She kissed at his chest and she smiled at his groan. She locked her leg around his hips. And felt her hips curl into his. This was perfect. She wanted to disappear into this dream, never wake up to the chaos her life had become. She wanted this to last forever but she had ruined everything. But one bite—he was so good she just wanted one bite of him.

"Hey! Easy with the teeth!"

Her eyes flew open as she scrambled off the bed. She landed on the floor on her butt, panting.

"What the hell are you doing here?"

The damn pirate smiled at her. "I was enjoying you kissing me, and I'd like to go back to that if you'll get your butt back in this bed?"

"I'm not... We didn't..."

"Mimi, look down. You are fully dressed and I don't have sex with barely conscious women, not even when they've got me hard as a rock." He lifted the covers to show that he was still wearing his cargo shorts and sporting a serious morning hard on. She dropped her eyes to her own clothes and while she was rumpled, he hadn't so much as unbuttoned a button.

"My butt is not going to be in a bed while you are in it. You still didn't answer the question— what are you doing here?"

"I'm the new tour sponsor. I'm someone you need to be nice to. I'm going to bring in the magic and turn this show into a happening."

She was having to fight off her body wanting to strip him naked and then tear her clothes off. Odd, since her sex drive had disappeared in the last two months. Not even a kinky dream since she was sleeping like hell. She shook her head to clear it of the thoughts his smile was putting there. *Great, like this job wasn't hard enough.* Now she was going to have to do it while keeping him happy without indulging in thoughts of Mr. Happy. Her life officially sucked.

"Okay, Mr. Tolland, would you like some coffee? Yes? Okay, I'll run right out and get some." She stood up and bolted for the door and out of the bus. Thankfully, they were playing two shows here before everything had to move next

and last night had been the first. She had
already found the best coffee in town, or what
passed for coffee on the East Coast.

She stood in line at the Coffee Clutch,
looking at her feet. Maybe no one else would
notice. In her mad dash, she had grabbed two
different shoes; in the state she was in, she was
happy she had managed a left and a right. An old
woman walked past and Mimi smiled at her.

"Tough night last night, honey?" The woman
grinned at her and chuckled. Mimi felt herself
blush to her toes; she could just imagine what
she looked like. "If I were you, I'd hang on to a
man that could make me look like that."

The woman sat at a table with her coffee and
honeybun. Mimi suddenly missed her parents
horribly. Her mom would have been younger
than this woman by at least twenty years or so.
She ordered the coffees and decided she had
nothing to lose.

"Mind if I join you for a second?" Mimi sat
down without waiting for an answer. If the last
two months had taught her anything, it was how
to be more assertive. "How did you know I was
with a guy?"

The old woman looked up from her book. "I
suppose I didn't but you have that ruffled, loved-

up look and there was something in your eyes. Forget it; it is none of my business."

"No, I was. He makes me crazy."

The woman smiled and got a faraway look in her eyes. "Mmm, I remember that. Makes you want to either throw things or tear his clothes off."

"Yes! But how do I know it isn't just sex?"

"You kids! What the hell is wrong with sex? Relationships have been built on worse things. If he is good to you and behaves, not gambling away all your money, or drinking it, what is wrong with being good in the sack?"

Mimi snapped her mouth shut. She had wanted to talk to someone and this woman was a pistol.

"But he lied to me."

"Oh, married already?"

"No! He's...He's rich, I mean, like, stinking rich."

The woman stared at her for a good twenty seconds.

"So let me get this straight: he is hot in bed, and stinking rich? Sweetheart, if you don't want him, can you send him my way?"

"No, you don't understand. He let me think he was a starving artist."

"And he's got no talent? What?" The woman was looking at her like she was not all there mentally.

"No, actually he's tremendously talented. He just has this company that makes money like crazy."

"Honey, you might be a smart girl in other things but you are dumb as a stump when it comes to men. Sorry, at my age you get a little blunt."

"No, you're right, I am. So I should just go back there and finish, um, what we started."

"Or tell him to look up Mrs. Grace Camenitti in Boston. I like younger guys and at my age they're all younger."

"Okay, I'll let him know if it doesn't work out."

"Relax, sweetheart; he'd be crazy to leave you."

Mimi tossed her coffee and made her way back to the bus with his. She walked in to find the bus empty or at least Eric missing in action. Her sister was still asleep but then she usually slept till at least noon. Where the hell could he be? She felt like a fool walking around with a coffee and not drinking it. She'd just have to find him.

She had been searching for half an hour, the coffee long ditched since it was now cold. *Had she just dreamed him?* She felt like she was losing her mind when she walked between two tractor trailers, finding him with some tiny little hard body wrapped around him.

"So, must have missed me a bunch?"

"Mimi. Um, this isn't what it looks like," he said over the girl's shoulder.

"Of course not. Most women you meet wrap their legs around your waist." She turned on her heel and walked away. *Mrs. Cama whatever could have him.* Suddenly, she was yanked back between the trucks.

"Hey, I'm serious. That was not what you thought it was. She was just a kid. Someone I helped out a while ago. She's like maybe twenty and not exactly my type."

"Eric, I've seen the press clippings. She is exactly your type. We've been through this and nothing has changed." She tried to get away from him but he pinned her against the truck with his body.

"Oh no, you listen to me. She was Rik Toil's type and yes, he has a thing for skater girls. He has to. I don't. I like a woman with some substance. With a little fire in her, a little sass.

You have all of that in spades, though you are flirting with being taken over my knee." She sucked in a breath. *He wouldn't dare?* At the same time she thought, *hell yes, he would.* "I like a woman that is soft and melts when I whisper in her ear. I only have eyes for my angel and you are it."

"Eric, I am..."

He kissed her so she couldn't say more. He pulled away.

"I didn't get a chance to do that this morning. And damn, I really wanted to. Angel, do you know how many women I've been out with since you walked out of my office?" *She really didn't need to know this, not now, not the way she was feeling.* "Exactly zero. See, when I said I own all of your orgasms, I cursed myself because you seem to own all of mine."

She stopped struggling to get away for a second. It took a little longer for that to sink in. She didn't think he was the type to immediately pick up another girl. *But none?*

"No one?"

"Not just no one; didn't even want to till I saw you sleeping on the couch last night and then, well, I ended up cursing my mother up one side and down the other but when you started running your hands over me this morning...You've cursed me. I only want you, Mimi."

She ducked her head; his fingers curled around her chin and lifted her face to his.

"Angel, tell me the truth. Have you...Has anyone..."

"God, no! I...The band is all girls and the roadies are well, roadies and...I didn't even want to."

"And now?"

"Eight weeks of bottled up hormones and I feel like a damn teenager."

He smiled. "Good. Hate to think I was in this alone."

"Eric, can we start over? I mean from the beginning."

"What was wrong with the time we were together?"

"Nothing!" She blushed, thinking of the things they had done in the time they were together. "Nothing. But, we just kinda jumped into bed and never really got out."

The damn pirate smile was back and her body reacted like she'd been zinged with a cattle prod. "Mmm, good times." He got a glazed look to his eyes.

"Stop! That is what I am talking about. Okay, the sex thing works—okay, it works really well. But are we even friends? I mean, really? Eric, we live in such different worlds."

"You mean would I come bail you out in the middle of the night? Mimi, I'd give you a kidney if you needed it. You're mine, my angel. I don't know how to explain it to you except to say that with other women, it was physical or even less—sorry, but you wanted the truth. With you, even arguing with you is better than the best sex I had before I met you. And yes, it scares the hell out of me. But I don't want to lose this so if you need to spend some time as just friends, I can do that but I need something in return."

She threw her arms around him.

"Anything. Oh, thank you."

"You haven't heard what I want yet."

"Um, I don't have to pierce or tattoo anything, do I?"

He laughed and she joined in.

"No, worse." She stopped laughing. "You want to be friends and I want you in my bed."

She started to shake her head but he grabbed her chin and made her nod yes instead.

"The whole idea is to remove sex from the equation."

"Angel, the only time sex is out of the equation for you and I is when one of us is dead. I am going to want you when we are old, when you are round with my baby and your feet are so swollen your shoes don't fit, when..."

"I get the idea! So we are going to sleep, just sleep, in the same bed till I'm satisfied we really could live in the same world?"

"Or till you give in to my pirate charm." Her mouth dropped open. "Yeah, you talk in your sleep. I was starting to get a little freaked last night when you kept mumbling about your sexy pirate till you said my name."

She wanted to wipe the smug grin off his face. "How do you know I wasn't trying to get away from you?"

"Because when I leaned in and kissed you, you purred and whispered you missed your pirate, and you wouldn't let me go. You want me." She punched his chest, not hard enough to really hurt him but it got him to let her go. "You can fight it all you want but you are sleeping in my bed tonight or...actually, there is no 'or'—so decide whether it will be with your clothes on or off. I'm not going to force you to do anything you don't want but I reserve the right to make you want to change your mind."

She was reduced to growling at him. "You don't even have a place to sleep!"

"I will by this afternoon. Go get your work done." He spanked her on the butt to send her on her way. She stuck her tongue out over her shoulder and headed back to the bus. She needed a shower and a change of clothes—oh, and shoes that matched!

She had seen Eric take delivery of the deluxe motorhome. He looked at her and saluted with the receipt. Her stomach did the roller coaster thing. *How the heck was she going to do this unless she got him to cave first?* She gave the idea a little thought; it just might work. He'd give up and let her go back to her own bed if he was so frustrated that he couldn't think straight.

She smiled and the smile kept getting bigger. Of course, she was going to be mighty frustrated too, but she could outlast him; she was sure of it. This might even be fun. She couldn't remember the last time she had teased some guy; actually, she didn't think she ever had. No guy she had ever known before had made her feel like she had something they wanted this badly. Maybe the old lady at the coffee shop wasn't so crazy. If it all fell apart, she was going to have a lifetime of great sex and unlimited devotion, according to him. She really was an idiot but what the heck, she owed him a little torture for lying to her.

She picked out her clothes more carefully than usual. She had decided on the brocade jacket when her sister walked in, drying her hair.

"Mimi, I think...Wow, would this outfit have anything to do with a certain skateboarder who wormed his way in to sponsoring the tour?"

"Um, too obvious? I should change."

"Not a chance in hell. It is good to see you in something other than the depression clothes you've been wearing. Where did you get the boots?"

Mimi looked down at the designer version of biker boots and smiled. With the heels and platform on these, she was over six feet tall. They made her feel powerful, even if he still would be a couple inches taller than her.

"The same store I got the corset. There is a local leather shop that had some great pieces."

"I never figured I'd see you in a leather corset but it looks great, especially with the jacket."

The jacket was Mimi's favorite piece. Heavy brocade and velvet played up her curves; it looked like she had torn it off a pirate. Maybe it would give her pirate some ideas? There was a knock on the door of the bus. She fluffed her hair in the mirror and ran her tongue over her teeth to get any lipstick off.

She didn't know what to expect when she opened the door but a grown man staring at her with his mouth open was not it. Unfortunately, it wasn't the man she was hoping for. Carl, one of the roadies, just stood, blinking. Mimi suddenly had the feeling that if she had asked him to bark like a dog he would have barked and started chasing his tail.

"Carl? Is there a problem?"

He managed to swallow. *Okay, his reflex reactions were working.*

"Carl!"

"Wha...Oh, shit. Damn!"

Oh goody, he can speak.

"Was there a reason you are here?"

"Oh, yeah. I'm supposed to give you this." He handed her an envelope with her name on it. He was starting to make her feel uncomfortable now with the way he was staring.

"Was there anything else?"

"Uh, no." He wasn't leaving, though.

"Okay. Can you make sure the lighting guys have the corrected set list?"

"Sure, anything! I'll get right on it." He tripped on the way down the steps but caught himself before he outright fell. He turned around and walked away backwards, looking at her with a dumb smile the whole time. When she turned around, Audi was behind her.

"Oh my God, you ruined another one."

"What?"

"Forget it. The note from lover boy?"

"Oh, I haven't opened it yet." She tore it open and read.

Your pirate requests the honor of your presence on his ship (of sorts) for dinner
Plan on being dessert!
See you as soon as the band goes on. Tell your sister not to wait up.
E

A shiver ran up her spine. This didn't exactly feel friendly but it was probably as close as the pirate was going to get.

"Eric just wants to get together for dinner. You won't need me once the show starts, will you?"

"No, he'll have no idea what hit him. I'd tell you to have fun but I think it would be redundant at this point."

"Um, yeah, about that? Um, I'll probably sleep there."

"I figured. Shit, I have to get myself together if we are going to start on time."

"Need any help?"

"No, I should be good. Go stalk your boyfriend."

"Audi!"

Her sister turned her back and ran to get dressed.

Forty-five minutes later, she stood on the step of the motorhome, knocking on the door.

"Permission to come aboard?"

Eric pulled the door open and she pushed past him. If he acted like a jerk, she was out of here. Suddenly, guys she had seen every day for the last few weeks were turning into morons and she'd had enough. The inside of the coach was all rich wood paneling. It would be easy to imagine they were in the belly of a ship. Everything gleamed and was beautifully organized, definitely captain's quarters except for the new-car smell. She never got why guys loved it so much.

She turned around to smile at him and stopped.

"Eric, what's wrong? Am I too early for dinner? You said to come by when they went on."

Mother of Hell! What had happened to his angel? Breathe, man! Don't panic. Cool, be cool.

"The hell with dinner!" he growled at her. *So much for cool.* He backed her toward the bedroom.

"Eric! You promised—no sex."

"Are you fucking kidding me? You show up looking like..." He took in the boots with the jeans tucked into them, making her legs look like they went on for miles. The coat was coming off right now if he had his way, but the way it flared out over her hips made her look like a comic book vixen and made his knees weak. Then there was the damn corset. *Shit!* Black leather, simple but perfect; he was going to have so much fun getting her out of that. His fingers itched to start unlacing her now.

"Like what?"

"Like you were trying to make a man fall to his knees and beg."

"This is supposed to be a friendly dinner."

"Friends show up in sweats; friends don't wear 'Catch 'Me' boots. Friends wear their hair in a boring ponytail, not in some soft sweet-

smelling cloud to trap a man in. And friends
don't wear lipstick made to give a man fantasies
about..."

"Oh, I, I thought I looked nice; I'll go change
if you want."

"Angel, if you take a single piece of this off, I
want a damn ticket to the show."

"I'm confused. It stays or goes?"

"*You* stay; *it* can go later. I did warn you you'd
be dessert, right?" He watched as she shivered.
He loved that little shiver. "Come here."

She smiled shyly, completely at odds with the
in-charge attitude of the clothes. He held his
arms out to her and she walked into them. She
was taller in the heels. He rested his forehead
against hers when he wrapped her in his arms.

"I look okay?"

"So, so much better than okay, babe. I am not
letting you out of here in that, just so you know."

"I was promised dinner."

He stole a kiss and tried to get the blood back
up to the other head. He pulled in a deep breath
and blew it out hard.

"Dinner coming up. Why don't you sit while I
serve?" He had set the tiny table so that they
were sitting next to each other on the banquette;
maybe that wasn't such a good idea now. *Shit, she*

couldn't be serious about the no sex thing, could she?
He looked over at her and knew she was dead
serious. He was so fucked and not in the way he
wanted to be. She was a damn demon, not an
angel. He pulled the sliding door half closed to
hide the take-out cartons and put all the food on
the plates—South Boston's finest Italian, hot
and fresh. His mouth watered at the eggplant
parm. At least that is what he told himself.

"Here you go, angel. I hope you like chicken
parmesan. There is a Caesar salad, no anchovies,
too, if you want to start with that?"

"The chicken is fine." She seemed so shy now.
Kick-ass clothes or not, his angel was still there.
He breathed a sigh of relief. He poured the wine
and left it on the table to breathe and then slid
in next to her. He reached over, pulling her in
close.

"There, much friendlier." He left his arm
around her waist. "Wait a sec. You don't want to
get any sauce on your coat. Why don't you give it
to me?"

"Oh, I suppose you're right."

He helped her take the jacket off and forgot
how to breathe for a second—or maybe more.
Everything swam before his eyes before he could
pull himself back together. He couldn't believe

the woman of his dreams was sitting here in a leather corset like it was no big deal.

"Oh, I just realized, I mean I probably shouldn't have worn leather, I mean, you're vegetarian."

"Mostly because I can't cook to save my life. Undercooked vegetables are just extra crunchy; they won't make you sick." She looked suspiciously at the food on her plate. "Um, okay, I had this couriered to me from Boston. I can handle reheating." The relief on her face made him smile. "Besides, leather is a byproduct of the meat industry and if you are going to kill the cow, may as well make use of all of it." His appetite for food had disappeared when the coat came off. All that creamy soft skin was making his mouth water. He offered up a silent prayer but if prayers like that were answered, being a teenage boy would have been a lot more interesting.

He turned into a believer when about fifteen minutes into the meal she was talking with a bite of food on her fork. There may have been just a little too much sauce or he had done some good deed that called for a reckoning of the karmic balance. Whatever it was, he looked at the drip of red sauce laying just above the top of the corset like it was the keys to the kingdom. Mimi reached for her napkin and he batted her hand away.

"I got it." He leaned toward her and caught her eye. The woman was holding her breath. He bent his head and licked at the sauce. He closed his eyes when the first shiver ran through her. He couldn't resist, the damn woman was like a drug. He sucked harder and brought the blood to the surface. Not enough to really give her a love bite but she could definitely feel it. Since he had her distracted, he popped the top snap or whatever that thing was on the corset. He ran his finger through the sauce on his plate and lifted her breast with his other hand. He painted her nipple with his finger and watched as her eyes half closed.

"Oops." He bent his head and sucked her nipple into his mouth. He was rewarded with her hiss and that damned addictive shiver. Then he felt her melt. He looked up into her eyes; they were half closed and he heard her sigh. His breath caught. This was different than she had done before. It was as if the last of her resistance was gone and she was finally all his.

He swallowed hard in response to the trust she was giving him. He kissed his way up her cleavage to her creamy shoulders and neck.

"Mimi, talk to me."

"Hmm?"

"Talk to me, angel."

"Can't. Need you." Her voice was thick with desire, which just made what he was about to do harder. Her hand came up to pull him to her lips but he stopped her.

"My sweet angel, I need you to understand what you are doing."

"Eric." Her voice had turned to a growl.

"I want you to come with me." He took her hand and led her to the bedroom. When he got there, he sat her on the bed and pulled out one of his T-shirts and a pair of sweatpants. "Put these on."

She seemed to snap back into herself at the request.

"Those will never fit me."

"I say they will and I want you to put them on. Now." The request had become a demand and she still hesitated. He stared her down. She finally started removing her boots. "Would you like some privacy?"

"Yes, please." Her voice was barely audible. He held his smile in check.

"Call me when you are done." He walked out and closed the door. He tapped his foot for seven minutes till she said she was dressed. When he walked in, she was trying to hide herself behind her arms. "Arms at your sides." She looked at him and he thought for a minute she might burst into tears. She closed her eyes and willed her arms down. He opened the closet door so that he could use the full-length mirror. He pushed past her and cradled her back against his front.

"Open your eyes, Mimi. I want you to see how perfectly we fit together." She turned and looked over her shoulder at him. He gently turned her to face the mirror in front of them.

She still fought looking in the mirror.

"Stubborn angel, we'll be here all night this way. Look, dammit." There was more frustration, for one good reason, in his voice than true anger. He wrapped his arms around her waist and started kissing her shoulder where the skin peeked out of the T-shirt. She relaxed in his arms and he finally got her to look in the mirror.

"First, do you know how great it is just that I can do this? A simple thing like wrapping my arms around your waist and not having to bend myself into some damn pretzel makes me feel like I want to do it all the time. Would you have a problem with that?"

"With you holding me like this?" He nodded yes and went back to nibbling her shoulder. "Oh," it came out as a whimper, "no, I guess not. But I..." Her arms came up to hide her breasts.

"Arms down."

"But the shirt is too tight and I'm...droopy."

"Angel, you have big shoulders and large breasts that I love to feel fill my hands. I have big hands. If your breasts were tiny, they wouldn't fit you and you wouldn't fill my hands, wouldn't weigh anything on my tongue, wouldn't pillow my head when I listen to your heart beat." His hand moved from her waist to cup one of her breasts. His thumb teased her nipple; when she responded, he rolled it between his thumb and finger.

"Oh." Her head dropped to the side, baring her neck to him.

"And so responsive. God, you are mouth-watering," he whispered in her ear. She leaned against him, his hips thrust against her, grinding his erection into the top of her round rear end. He moved his other hand from her waist to slide over the curve of her hip as it traveled around to cup that full cheek. Her breath hitched.

"Angel, I don't like that you have lost weight, stubborn woman. I hate to think it is because of me. I want you to take care of yourself. I love the feel of this soft skin in my hands, feeling you so open and vulnerable. Sliding into you is heaven." She moaned. He eased back from her and held her around the waist again but this time like he was going to lift her. He dropped to his knees behind her, sliding his hands down the outside of her thighs. "I love that your legs are long and strong; God, I even love your pretty feet. I want to paint your toes sometime." That made her giggle. "After I've tied you to the bed, of course."

She stopped laughing.

"Damn pirate."

He smiled his most innocent smile back at her.

He stood up and circled his arms around her again. This time, she didn't shy away from looking in the mirror at the two of them.

"The outfit you walked in here wearing was sexy as hell but even like this you bring me to my knees. I just want you to see what I'm seeing when I look at you."

She turned in his arms so they were facing each other and kissed him. It was a kiss that showed him how much she loved him more than the words ever could.

"Make love to me, Eric."

He rubbed his lips along her hairline.

"Not yet. Get into bed." She started to slide the sweatpants off but he stopped her. "Better leave those on for now." She looked confused but he just pointed to the bed. He dashed out and grabbed her plate. The best thing about Italian food is it is still pretty good even when it was cold. He walked back in and almost laughed at the confused look on her face.

"I'm serious about you not losing more weight. I'm going to feed you before we do anything."

"Eric..."

"Not a word, angel." He sat on the bed and pulled a piece of chicken off. "Open up." She grimaced at him and crossed her arms over her chest. "We can make this a battle of wills and I will win, so make it easy on yourself. Open. Your. Mouth."

"Ugh, fine." She stuck out her tongue; he put the morsel of food there and she swirled her tongue around his fingers.

"Distracting me won't work, either."

"Damn."

He pulled off another piece. "Turn around and lay across my lap." She did what he asked and then grabbed a pillow to raise her head some. "Comfy?"

"Yes, thank you. You may proceed with the torture."

He lowered the bite of food to her lips but snatched it away when she tried to take it. He bent his head and kissed her instead. "Mmm, dessert."

She smiled.

He groaned. He'd gotten whipped cream and chocolate sauce just for tonight. But it didn't feel right now. He felt so protective of her. She was so full of contradictions, fighting him one minute and melting the next. She was starting to trust what he felt for her was real and outside of everything she thought about herself.

He proceeded to tease her, alternating bites of food and kisses till the chicken was done.

"That had to be the best meal I've ever eaten. But you didn't eat anything."

"No way. You are my captive—I am the Pirate King. I make the rules."

"Can I get one teensy little concession?" She was definitely up to no good. "Take your shirt off. I've missed your tattoos."

"I don't think that is such a good idea."

She put her arms around his neck and pulled him down to her lips but instead of kissing him, she whispered in his ear.

"I've missed that damn piercing of yours, too."

"That settles it. No way am I taking my shirt off."

"Why not?"

"Because I want to prove to you, you can depend on me and if I force you"—she smirked at him—"okay, convince you to have sex with me now, then I would be going back on my word."

"Even if I've changed my mind?"

"Especially if you've changed your mind. What's to say you don't change it back tomorrow and then you regret having sex with me again?"

"I don't regret having sex with you before. I just didn't like being lied to."

"Okay, so I am proving I am worthy of your trust. You said no sex, so no sex. You are sleeping in that and I am going to sleep in, well, the same thing, I guess. You are going to be in my bed, though. Last night was the first decent night's sleep I've had since you left."

"Me, too. Come on. I'll wash, you dry, and then I want to curl up together."

Should he be disappointed she was so happy they weren't having sex?

Ten minutes later, they were back in the bedroom but he didn't look happy. She looked at him and burst out laughing. He was soaking wet and had puffs of soap bubbles in his hair.

"A splash fight? Really? What are you, twelve?" he grumbled.

"Sore loser. Here, let me help." She stood in front of him and started to unbutton his shirt. With the first pop of the button, her whole body went soft. Her eyes suddenly felt heavy and she bit at her lip. She gave up and leaned against him. His arms wrapped around her with one hand cupping her ass. *The man did have big hands.*

"Angel, what is going through that dangerous mind of yours?"

"Um, my mind doesn't have much to do with this, Pirate King." She leaned forward and kissed at the skin she exposed. With each button, she repeated the sequence: pop, kiss, maybe a little lick. He was always so warm.

She pushed the sides of his shirt apart and admired the swirl of images there. She turned him so that his back was to the bed and pushed. He fell with a thud and then propped himself up on his elbows. She slid off his skater shoes. She reached for the baggy cargos he almost always wore. She looked up into his eyes as she undid the button at his hips and then slowly slid the zipper down. She couldn't resist anymore and glanced down. She tried to keep the smile off her face and failed utterly. He was hard as a rock.

"Well, what the hell did you think was going to happen?" He sounded exasperated.

"Are you angry with me?"

"Never for that, sweetheart. Just my lack of control around you, that's all." He reached up and cupped her face in his hand. She backed away and looked down at him.

"Shorts on or off?"

"What?"

"If you are going to sleep in sweats, do you want your shorts on or off?"

"Off, I guess."

"Living dangerously?" She reached over to open the drawer he'd pulled the clothes for her out of. She pulled out a tank and cut-off sweatpants. At least she'd get to see some of him. When she turned back, he had an odd look on his face. "What?"

"Nothing, I just...forget it."

She reached down and ran her hand down his stomach and watched his eyes droop and a shiver run through his body. *Her pirate liked being taken care of.* Well, she was just getting started. He reached for the clothes but she snatched them away.

"Oh no, I'm your captive, remember? This is my job." She curled her fingers in to the elastic of his shorts. She watched as he took a very deliberate breath. She eased the elastic over his erection and slid it down his ass. He still had his shirt covering his arms but he looked so decadent. She tossed the clothes on the bed and went to the bathroom. She found a washcloth and ran it under the hot water.

When she came back, he tried to get up but she straddled him. "Oh no, you don't. I get to take care of you this time." She ran her hand through his hair; it was like silk in her fingers. She bent and kissed his forehead and down his very patrician nose. Finally, she took his lips. She smiled against them when she heard him groan.

"You'll sleep better if you're clean. Lie back."

He seemed to collapse back onto his elbows. She settled herself over him, reaching the warm cloth to the back of his neck. He closed his eyes. Her jungle cat had turned in to a big ol' pussy cat. She washed down his chest. She bit her lip when she washed over his nipples and he sucked in his breath. She leaned forward, trapping his erection between them and bit gently on one of his nipples.

"Angel, you are playing with fire."

"Just testing you and, well, I can't help myself."

He slid his hands under the hem of the T-shirt, tracing his fingers over the swell of her breasts.

"Can't seem to help myself, either."

She moved down his body, trailing the cooling damp cloth after her. Finally, she kneeled on the floor, stroking his thighs, watching as goose bumps broke across his skin. She smiled at him and dropped the damp cloth over his erection. He hissed at the cold on his hot skin.

"I never did get even for that ice thing you did." She massaged him lightly through the material while he took deep gulps of air. When he opened his eyes, they were dark as the ocean. She inched away. "Oh, shit," she mumbled under her breath. "Eric, you said we weren't going to..."

"Strip."

"But you said..."

"I said you were playing with fire but you kept throwing gas on the flames."

"Eric..."

"Strip!"

She lifted the hem of the shirt but she must not have moved fast enough so he grabbed at the V neck and tore it down the middle. Oh shit, she had been turned on before but now she was panting. Her heart was pounding in her chest.

"Wha...What are you going to do!"

"Angel, I've hurt you more than I ever wanted to when I lied to you. I won't ever hurt you again, you know that, right?" She nodded; she wasn't afraid of him. He just looked so intense right now. He slid toward her and guided her onto the bed. "These need to come off, too." He yanked on the sweatpants till they were around her ankles and she kicked them off her feet. He sat back for a second and stared down at her. Finally, she started shivering but not from the cold. She tried to cover herself but he stopped her.

"Never hide from me. Got it? There is nothing about your body I don't find amazing and beautiful. Nothing." She gripped the covers to keep her hands by her sides. "Good girl. When you finally believe me, it won't be so hard. Now, you had your fun. It is my turn."

"Bu...But you said you wouldn't have sex with me."

"If you mean I am going to deny myself the unbelievable pleasure of sliding into your amazing body? Then yes, we are not going to have sex. But if you think I am going to let you get away with teasing me and then I'll just roll over and go to sleep, you are dead wrong, my little captive." Her pirate was back, big time. "Now, I am going to tease you." Her body seemed to relax against her will. He ran his fingertips over her everywhere like he was weaving a spell. After a couple of minutes, her body reacted if he even moved his hand over her without touching her skin. When he stretched himself out on top of her, it was overwhelming. He was holding his weight off her, just barely touching but after the teasing, it made her gasp. Her hips curled toward him.

"Eric, please..."

He nipped her ear and quietly said no. He pushed back and ran his lips over her nipples. They got harder and her whole chest seemed to rise, seeking his attention. He sucked open-mouth kisses all over her breasts and down her ribs. It tickled till he got to the place over her diaphragm. There he sucked harder, giving her a love bite.

"Hey! What are you doing?"

"What does it look like? I'm marking you as mine."

Maybe she should have been upset at how primitive it sounded but mostly she was turned on and collapsed back on the bed as he kissed his way down her belly. She expected him to keep going, so she was surprised when he stopped. He slipped his arms under her thighs, using his shoulders to open her up to him. Instinctively, she tried to close her legs.

"Hey! What did I say?"

"Never hide from you."

"Right. This is the essence of what makes you feminine. I'll be damned if I don't get to see this, too." He reached around and stroked the insides of her thighs. *Oh, that felt so good.* "Now for trying to hide, I think a little punishment is order." She might have been scared but his smile was playful, not intense, though his eyes were still that deep ocean color. He trailed more kisses up the inside of her thighs and then started giving her light love bites till he got almost to her pussy. That one was not light; actually, it stung and was dark compared to the others. She gasped at the sensations.

"What was that for?"

"Punishment and a warning to anyone that gets close to you that you are taken."

"You are the only one getting that close to me."

"Oh, I believe you. It is just the pirate in me —can't help myself."

It would have been cute if he didn't do the same thing on the other thigh. When she realized what was going to happen, she could at least prepare herself for the sting. She looked down to see the matching circles on her thighs and then at the grinning man who put them there.

"Well, at least they're high enough that I can still wear a skirt."

"Mmm, watch it. I like the idea of leaving my mark on you only I get to see."

"Eric, make love to me. Please?"

"No, angel. I was serious about what I said: as long as we are on this tour, no intercourse. Outercourse is a whole other story, though."

"Outercourse? You just made that up."

"No, there are whole books on it. But I can teach you everything you need to know. I'll make the first lesson easy: mutual masturbation."

"I'm not..."

"You touch me, I touch you. Trust me, it is way more fun than the other kind."

Forty-five minutes later, she was a puddle of sweat and so thoroughly sated she didn't think she could move. Eric walked back from the bathroom with a big grin on his face. He pulled on the cut-off sweatpants, bent to kiss her and then handed her a T-shirt. She looked at him and groaned.

"See, not so bad? Stunning orgasm and a feeling of accomplishment."

She pulled the hair away that was stuck to her face.

"You are truly twisted."

"Says the woman that was screaming so loud the people getting out of the concert could hear her."

She groaned and hid her face with the shirt.

"Come on. Did you want to take a quick shower or did you want me to wash you?"

"I don't think I can walk, you damn pirate."

"See, now you are just stroking my ego. Okay, sponge bath it is."

He had bathed her and dressed her with such tenderness that she ached. Then he slid into bed behind her, spooning her against him. If possible, she relaxed even more.

"I love you, Eric."

"Love you, too, Mimi."

"Tell me a story."

"Wanna hear the one about the geeky guy who was afraid to talk to girls?"

She managed to turn over and nuzzled her face into his chest.

"Definitely."

"In sixth grade, he shot up to over six feet tall. Everyone told him he should play basketball. Except he sucked at sports. The girls used to beat him at hockey. Everybody thought he was gay, which he wasn't. He kept a low profile in high school. Hung out in the art room, would have lived there if they let him. Got into college and decided being him sucked, so he would be someone else. The cool graffiti artist guy that girls actually wanted to be with. So he got some,

uh, training, hated most of it but he did feel
more confident talking to women. Got himself all
tatted up so he had something to hide behind
even when he was naked. And he worked his ass
off to get rich. Except when he should have been
enjoying the bennies of doing all that, the sex
felt empty, the work just meant having more
stuff, and he felt hollow. Then he ran into this
girl."

Mimi wrapped her arms tight around him
and pushed them so that he was on his back and
she was on top of him.

"It freaks you out I see the shy boy still in
you, doesn't it?"

"I'm trying to get used to it."

"So here's a different story. There was this
shy girl but she was trapped in this huge body.
Okay, maybe huge is overstating it but she felt
that way. She hid in the library, poring through
magazines. She thought if she could figure out
what made the people in the ads so happy then
she could be like them. She wasn't a great artist
but she was good at telling stories with pictures
and so she became one of the people making the
ads with the happy people. She was still shy, only
now she knew the people in the ads weren't any
happier than anyone else. Then she met the most

amazing man. What made him amazing is, he had an unescapable heart. Once he took you in, you never wanted to leave. It didn't hurt that he had a rogue's charm and good looks." She kissed him softly on the lips.

"Angel, don't ever leave me again. I don't think I could survive."

"Is that why you keep marking me?"

He suddenly looked like the five-year-old with his hand in the cookie jar.

"That obvious?"

"Uh huh. You are off the hook for now, though, since despite my better judgment it seems to turn on the shy high school girl still trapped inside me. The cool skater dude wants everyone to know I'm his." She couldn't have hidden her smile if she wanted to. "In a purely primal way, it is very sexy." He flipped them so she was under him now.

"I'm very happy to satisfy your base primitive urges, angel."

"Good. Because right now I desperately need sleep."

He rearranged them so they were spooned together again.

"'Night, my precious angel."

"Good night, my wicked pirate."

She fell asleep with him chuckling in her ear and kissing her neck.

Chapter Eight

Eric nearly jumped out of his skin when the light flicked on. *What the hell!* He tried to peel one eye open and gave up. Finally, he resigned himself to reaching out blindly. He felt that he was alone in the bed and frowned. He heard a plate and silverware being put down behind him on the built-in bedside table. *Oh thank God, he smelled coffee.*

"This may be a deal-breaker," he growled.

"What are you talking about?"

"You can't seriously be a morning person, angel?"

"Hmm, sorry, have been my whole life. Drove Audi nuts. But I ran to the store and stocked your kitchen with the basics and I come bearing breakfast and coffee."

He rolled to his back with his arm covering his eyes. "I don't think I can eat this early."

"Sure you can. Open." He did and she put a forkful of buttery scrambled eggs in his mouth. He chewed and swallowed. *That was surprisingly good.* "Open again." This time it was toast with lots of butter and strawberry jam. When some of the jam dripped at the corner of his mouth, she licked it off and he groaned. Nothing like a morning hard on made worse by a hot woman.

"Coffee," he croaked.

"That you'll have to sit up for." He pushed up and back to prop himself against the wall and finally opened his eyes. He blinked a few times but the picture didn't change. She sat on the edge of the bed with the plate in her lap, looking so happy to see him he wanted to dump everything on the floor and haul her back into bed.

"Your coffee, Captain." She grinned at him and he was sure he had a stupid grin on his face, too. He took a gulp, expecting the worst.

"How did you get real coffee? I mean, I've been out here for weeks and no one on the East Coast really knows how to make coffee."

"I had grabbed my French press when I came out to meet Audi and then saw she had her own. I pulled out mine when I picked up a bunch of my clothes." She suddenly looked shy.

He put the coffee down and held out his arms to her. "Come here, angel." She just about leapt on to him. "I wanted you here, I still want you here, but knowing you can make great coffee seals the deal." She popped him in the chest. "So is breakfast in bed a common thing for you? Because I don't remember that from before."

"You were never around in the morning. It wasn't like you skipped out exactly but it would have been nice to wake up together. We've never had morning sex."

"Morning sex?"

"Mmm, yeah, when you're all sleepy and warm—and you're already relaxed—it is that much better. But you would take off in the middle of the night." Now it was his turn to duck his head. "What? Oh God! If you tell me you were seeing someone else..."

"No! It was just—I had a company to run and I was spending all my time thinking about getting you into bed."

"You're twisted."

"Hey! You were the one talking about morning sex. What time is it, anyway?"

"Seven thirty."

"In the morning! Are you crazy? You've already showered, changed, gotten clothes, shopped for food, and made breakfast. What the hell time do you get up?"

"Five thirty. Rose usually has to go out by then."

"Hey, where is my other favorite girl?"

"Staying at the neighbor's. She's in love with their male miniature pincher. I've tried to tell her it will never work out but she's a romantic."

"I like the way she thinks."

She kissed him.

Mornings were starting to rise in his list of favorite parts of the day.

"When is your driver getting here so we can get going? 'The 'circus,' as you call it, pulls out in an hour or so, in order to get to Hartford in time to set up."

"He's here. You're looking at him."

"Eric, you can't be serious?"

"That was why I went with the motor home instead of a tour bus. This I can drive myself and I don't have to share you with anyone else."

"Uh, genius, if you had a driver we could be back here fooling around instead of you stuck up front driving. And how are you going to drive all day and then manage the event you have planned for the concert?"

"First off, if I had my way, no other guy would even get to look at you. And secondly, I've done this before; it will be fine."

"First off, you sound like a completely possessive freak when you say stuff like that and damn you for making me go all tingly when you do. Secondly, when was the last time you did this? I don't want to have to say I told you so."

***

Eric jerked awake. The Dan Ryan Expressway was not the place to be caught napping, especially if you were at the wheel. Dammit, he was tired. Mimi was right, not that he'd admit that to her. The last time he'd done this he'd been in his twenties and could survive on Red Bull and doughnuts. Of course, he'd had more motivation then, trying to prove his company could be a player in an already crowded market. And he hadn't had any distractions.

The thought made him smile. She was so much more than a distraction. A car horn warned him he had strayed from his lane. *Shit, get your head out of your ass, Tolland!* Thank God,

Mimi was safe in the bus with her sister. He hadn't wanted to let her go but she had said she had show stuff to discuss and then whispered the naughty things she wanted to do when she saw him tonight. He just needed to not get himself killed getting there.

When he pulled in, he was hoping to get some sleep but there were issues with the space they had been allocated and some of the ramps needed to be changed around to fit. His riders were all young, so he felt more than a little responsible for them. Like most kids, they thought they were invincible; it was up to him to make sure they stayed that way. He hadn't seen Mimi yet, but she had her own stuff to deal with as touring manager. He couldn't wait till this tour was over. He was hiring the band the best tour manager money could buy and keeping his angel in his bedroom for a week, maybe two. While they were there, she could plan their wedding. He'd give her anything she wanted. What he needed right now was more coffee if he was going to be able to check the scaffolding and then make it till tonight.

He was looking at the guys putting up the ramps when he felt cool, feminine hands slide over his eyes. He didn't know why but they didn't feel like Mimi's.

"Do I get a clue?" he asked.

"I know your deepest, darkest secrets," he got whispered back.

"That, I highly doubt, Eden."

"Dammit, I knew I should have disguised my voice."

He scooped her up in a hug. When he put her down, he took a good look at her. White blonde hair cut in a razor-sharp bob, had a body most women would kill for and she didn't have to do a thing for it, sparkly green eyes, and a sharp mind to top it all off. God, it was good to see her. He scooped her up again and swung her around. When he set her down this time, he faced a very ticked-off angel.

"Mimi, let me..."

"Explain? You can grovel later. Right now I want a word with 'little-miss-hands-all-over-my-'man' here." Eric bit the inside of his mouth to keep from laughing. He would have paid good money to see this and here he had a ringside seat for nothing.

"I don't think..." Eden tried to speak.

"Save it, sweetheart. I don't need to know what is going on. You just need to know that he is taken. Got it? He's mine. Take your tiny little body and go find someone more your size because you are just a snack and I am a whole buffet." *Okay, she was right about that.* He could swear he stood taller. All this time he'd been trying to get her to understand how great she was. Boy, when she went for it, she really went for it.

"Mimi, this is my sister Eden." His angel turned twelve shades of red and tried to run away. He managed to grab her before she got far. "Oh, no, you don't. That was fucking amazing! Gotta say, when you stake your claim on a guy, you don't hold back," he whispered in her ear while she buried her face in his chest. The woman was shaking. He rubbed her back for a minute to settle her. What a difference a couple of weeks made from when they were in Massachusetts. "Now come back here and meet my sister." He pulled her back to where Eden stood with a smile on her face.

"Obviously, my brother has been somewhat, difficult, to have a relationship with?"

"Hey! I'm a pussy cat." Mimi and his sister both looked at him like he was insane.

"I apologize. He, he's always surrounded by these skater girls and...I snapped. I'm sorry; I don't usually talk to people like that."

"I believe you. I'm Eden." His sister held her hand out.

"Mimi, seriously, I'm really sorry. Are you going to stay for the concert?"

"I don't know. Any cute guys in the band?"

"Um, sorry it's all girls."

"Figures. Sure, why the heck not? There have got to be guys that want to meet them, right?"

"Always! Ugh, fanboys. Come on, I'll introduce you to my sister and the rest of the group. You can hang out backstage."

"Angel, I've got some last minute checking to do and then I'll meet you back at the motor home so we can discuss exactly how you plan to stake your claim to me."

Mimi turned to Eden.

"He's never going to let me live that down, is he?"

"Not a chance. Wouldn't be my brother if he did."

Mimi lucked out and ran into Audi on her way backstage. She was happy to introduce Eden around, so Mimi walked back to find Eric. She could already picture the smug look on his face. She was sure he'd make some comment about not being able to stay away from him but in a way he was right. They were good together and after talking with Audi in the bus, she was more set on going back to Seattle. She missed her dog and making dinner in a kitchen that was bigger than a postage stamp. She wanted to be able to wake up and not have to remember where she was. And she wanted all of her man, all to herself. She was never going to be able to make it till the end of the tour. Maybe she should tell him that. He'd have them packed and on a plane in the hour.

She looked up at the big ramp and shuddered. She hated the thing; it looked like a death certificate waiting to happen, which was exactly the point. Eric had tried to explain all about big air and the rest of it but the thing gave her chills—and not the good kind. Someone was up there now but she couldn't make out who from this distance. She would just get Eric and get away from there. She couldn't bear to watch this part of the expo when it was going on.

As she got closer, she realized the rider wasn't one of the usual team members. She felt sick when she realized that it was Eric up there.

She started running but it wasn't like he would stop till he was ready. She watched as he dropped on to the ramp and started getting a rhythm going. His passes got longer and longer till he was flying off the half-pipe at either end. *Okay, he was fine.* He knew what he was doing. *Deep breaths; this was going to be okay.* The thought had not sooner been formed than she watched in horror as he twisted oddly. Being so tall, his center of gravity was off. She screamed as he plummeted headfirst to the ramp from at least forty feet up. She was stunned as he slid down to the bottom of the curve like a rag doll. Her heart beat wildly in the half a second she waited for him to move but there was nothing.

Other people started to climb on the ramp to get to him and she managed to get someone to call an ambulance.

"Don't move him! Don't even touch him!" she screamed. He could have a broken neck; he most certainly had a concussion. She scrambled on to the ramp and checked his breathing. *Thank God that was okay.* She checked his pupils but she didn't really know what she was looking for. She started talking to him in a soothing voice.

"Stay with me, baby. I've got big plans for us tonight." As she spoke more, she barely thought about what; mostly she just wanted him to key into the sound of her voice. As she spoke, she stroked his face and brushed her tears from his cheeks. The ambulance arrived and the paramedics got him into a collar and a backboard. She realized as she was getting into the ambulance she needed to let Audi know where she was and have her tell Eden to meet them at the hospital.

***

He was underwater. He had to get to the surface, had to get to his angel. She had promised to be his; he couldn't let her down. He clawed at the water, trying to break the surface. He was pulled back down. Again and again, he tried till he collapsed, exhausted.

When he tried again, the water was less murky, less cold. He couldn't move his arms. Would his angel love him enough to come to him? Again, cold ran through his veins and everything turned black.

His face was wet. Warm rain was dripping on him but light, like tears. Eric opened his eyes for

195

the first time in Twenty-four hours and saw an angel, more specifically his angel. His lids were heavy but he needed to get her to stop crying. *His angel shouldn't ever have to cry.* When he tried to speak, nothing came out but a hoarse croak.

"Water," he finally managed to say. Her eyes went wide and her smile beamed.

"Let me just tell the nurse that you are awake. I'll find out if you can have some ice or something." She ran out of the room and then came back, dragging a nurse with her.

"Yes, he can have ice chips." Mimi left again while the nurse checked the machines that were next to him. In seconds, Mimi was back with a large cup of ice. She placed a piece on his lips and then pushed it into his mouth. *God, nothing had ever felt so good.* The nurse left. Mimi quickly leaned over and kissed him. *Check that, kisses were much better than ice.* She pulled away and smiled at him. He closed his eyes for a second to remember that smile always.

"Eric!" His eyes snapped open. "Oh, God, I thought you were going back under." The tears were back.

"Angel. Don't. Cry." His voice was barely above a whisper. His words seemed to make the tears worse and she crumpled on his chest, sobbing. He wanted to soothe her. Needed to, in truth. But he couldn't get his hands to move. When she saw him struggling, she lifted her head and untied his hands.

"You kept trying to fight everyone off, so they had to restrain you. You need to promise to behave."

When she had finished, she moved back to his chest and he buried his hands in her hair. Finally, she cried herself out. He stroked her hair and back as much to reassure him as her. She looked at him with teary eyes and started kissing his cheeks, his forehead, eyes, and lips in a fury. Whatever had happened, he'd do it again if she would keep doing that.

"Do you remember anything that happened?"

"Don't know, really." He coughed and she fed him more ice. Which made him think of the time he'd showed her the possibilities of ice. Which brought parts of him back from the dead. Her breath caught when she realized what was going on. *Damn, he had so little control around this woman.* She pulled a round piece of ice from the cup and popped it in her mouth. She leaned over him, slowly pressing her lips to his as the ice dripped down into his mouth. It was hard to keep his eyes focused with her lips on his and his usual reaction to her. His pulse shot up and the machines started going crazy.

"Will you two break it up? The nurses are going crazy with the alarms."

Mimi pulled away from him and smiled at his sister's voice.

"He's awake."

"I guessed it was that or you were doing mouth to mouth."

Mimi gave Eden a big hug when she got next to the bed. His sister leaned over and kissed him on the forehead.

"You had your girlfriend pretty worried, big brother."

"Not you, though?"

"Nah, bump on the head? It's your least vulnerable spot."

He looked over at Mimi and wiped a tear from her cheek.

"Sorry I scared you."

"If you ever..." She huffed out a breath and Eric readied himself for a long lecture. "No, I swore to myself, I wasn't going to do this. I love you and I just want you to get better so I can take you home."

"But the tour..."

"Will go on without us. I called Steve and he got someone to manage both the concert and the road show. The only thing you need to be responsible for now is getting better. And just so you know, I am in charge till you do. I am taking care of you, buster, not the other way around, got it?"

"Yes, 'ma'am." She lit up and he couldn't help smiling, too. "Eden, I don't suppose there is any chance you didn't call Mom?"

"I called her. Mimi talked to her, too."

He looked at Mimi and her grin had gotten bigger.

"Oh hell, what is going on now?"

"Eric Tolland, we are getting married. And no, I am not asking, I am telling you. I..."

"Yes."

"Really?" She looked like she was going to cry.

"Really, but don't start crying again because it breaks my heart to see you in tears." Big fat teardrops rolled down her cheeks anyway but the grin on her face at least let him know they were happy tears. "And can you let me believe that you asked me because of my overwhelming charm and not that you feel sorry for me after talking to my mother?"

"That woman thinks the sun rises and sets on you. I asked you to marry me because the last twenty-four hours have been hell and the thought of living without you...Eric, I love you and I want to spend the rest of my life showing you. Of course, you are going to need to play it a little safer to stick around long enough to find out just how much."

"Hey, since you're asking me does that mean you have to give me an engagement ring?"

"If she's smart, she'll put a ring through your nose."

"Eden!" both he and Mimi yelled.

"Just saying. Mimi, if you want to use my place to shower or you just need a break from all the hospital stuff, here's the address. Seriously, congratulations, guys."

"Why don't you look happy?" Mimi asked.

"I'm going be the only one not married and Mom is going to be absolutely single-minded now."

Eric laughed and then winced at the pain it caused.

Chapter Nine

Eric cracked open one eye. He was never going to naturally be a morning person but this particular morning there was no way he was sleeping late. Brushing aside her hair, he nuzzled the back of Mimi's neck. The last few months had been surreal with all the changes but so worth it. Mimi murmured in her sleep and he slid out of bed before she could wake up. Pajama pants had been one of the hardest changes to get used to but having a rock star show up in the middle of the night unannounced made it necessary. He walked out and met the rock star in question in the living room.

"You made it. Your sister was worried you wouldn't."

"Like I'd miss this."

"Yeah, your sister worries too much."

"And you don't ever give her anything to worry about?"

"Yeah, well, I'm working on it. I'm making coffee. Want any?"

"Oh yeah, I've been up since yesterday. When I decided I wanted to sing in front of people, I didn't quite understand I'd be giving up anything close to a normal life. I'm not even talking about the crazy fans either. I just would like to find a nice guy that wanted to get a pizza and spend the day in bed."

"Ugh, okay, this is a bit much first thing in the morning."

"No shit. Forget it, today is all about you guys. I just need some sleep or some sex, but neither of those are happening so I'll just make do with coffee."

A couple of minutes later, Eric snuck back into the bedroom with breakfast. He kissed his Cinderella and felt his chest swell with her instinctive reaction to him.

"Mmm, do I smell breakfast?"

"So it wasn't me you were reacting to?"

"Oh, you mean the way I pulled you in, the way my body unconsciously tries to wrap itself around you, or maybe the way my heart beats faster? No, that is just the way I react to scrambled eggs." She hit him with a pillow.

"Hey!" He bent to kiss her and then ducked lower to nibble her collarbone. "I don't love wearing pajama pants but I've gotta say, you wearing the tops, makes me want to pop the buttons off." To prove his point, he slid his fingers through the opening and undid the top few, kissing his way down her body.

"Um, don't get too involved there, mister."

"What? I want to make love to my girlfriend one last time."

"Yeah, where is she going?"

"She's getting married, becoming respectable; she won't want to hang out with the pirate anymore."

She started giggling and then it progressed to outright cackling till she had tears in her eyes.

"Oh, I think she'll always want her pirate and as far as being respectable, come here." Her eyes had softened as she reached for him. "I never was, where you are concerned," she whispered in his ear.

***

Mimi took a deep breath and blew it out hard.

"Last-minute nerves?"

"About marrying Eric? No."

"Actually, I meant the dress."

"Oh, no, not that either. I just wish Mom and Dad could have been here."

"I know." Both sisters were quiet for a second, and then Mimi threw her arms around Audi. "I'm so glad you made it, though."

"Anything for you, kiddo. It feels like everyone I know is getting married. And I can't even get laid!" She started cracking up while Mimi glared at her. "Sorry. I'm still punchy from lack of sleep. You ready to get this show on the road?"

"You bet."

Audi got them to start the music and Mimi mentally rehearsed the things she had written to say. Writing their own vows sounded like a great idea but was a lot harder than she thought it would be. How could she sum up what she felt about Eric, and in front of everyone, too? If she forgot everything, she would just tell him that she loved him forever. She fluffed out the skirt of her dress and smiled in the mirror.

The dress was plain thin muslin but yards and yards of it, held to her body with a corset made of leather straps, sort of like a harness right up to the brass ring just under the valley of her breasts. The leather made little pleats in the fabric so it wasn't as sheer as it started out. There were little puff sleeves that bared her shoulders and the back dipped almost to her waist. It was part Renaissance princess, part pirate captive. She had opted to go barefoot for the wedding. What was the sense of getting married outside if you couldn't feel the grass under your feet? Instead of a veil that would be murder in the wind on the bluff, she decided on a crown of wild flowers with her hair half up in front. She was retucking a few curls when Audi showed up again in the little cottage where she had gotten ready.

"Okay, we should get going. There are clouds coming in that look like they mean business." They locked arms and headed for the door. "Wait, Mimi. I want to say I'm really proud of you. I think Mom and Dad would have been, too. The last few months, seeing you with Eric and how you've dealt with everything...I think you

have really come into yourself. I'm going to have
to come up with a new nickname for you because
Mimi the Meek doesn't really fit anymore."

"Love you, too, you angry leprechaun. And
that nickname still fits! Come on, let's get me
married to my pirate."

"Dude, really—puffy shirts?"

"Steve, enough about the shirts! The music's
started. She is going to come out any minute."

"Nervous?"

"No."

The rest of the conversation died in their
throats when the girls walked arm-in-arm down
the aisle.

"Wow."

"Yeah." Eric swayed on his feet. Mimi looked
fierce and beautiful. His avenging angel.

"I meant...forget it."

"Did you say something?" He couldn't take
his eyes off her. His lungs hurt from holding his
breath. He pulled in as much air as he could. It
wasn't near enough to get his brain to work. He
couldn't remember a single thing he'd written to
say. Oh hell. *Think, Tolland!* It was hopeless; as
long as she was standing there looking like that,
he was done for.

Audi reached for his hand and put it in
Mimi's. It was ice cold so he grabbed the other
one, too, and started rubbing them while the
justice of the peace talked. Then it was his turn
to speak.

He looked at Mimi again. He was still
speechless. He hooked his finger in the brass
ring and pulled her closer. When even that
wasn't close enough, he wrapped her in his arms.
His fingertips traveled the tips of her spine
where his lips had kissed this morning and
would again tonight. He buried his nose in her
hair and finally the scent of her brought him
back to life. Just like she had when he first saw
her.

"The sight of you took all the pretty words I
was going to say. So I can only tell you what is in
my heart. Mine, Mimi. You are mine to love, to
honor, to cherish, to command"—which earned
him a smirk "and to obey, till the end of time.
You are precious to me." There were tears in her
eyes but also love and a smile on her lips so he
ducked his head and stole a quick kiss. The
Justice of the Peace cleared his throat. "Sorry,
couldn't resist."

Mimi said what she had prepared. He was so
caught up in the moment, he couldn't remember

what she had said when she finished. He hoped to hell someone was getting this. Finally, the JP said he could kiss the bride—again—which earned a laugh from everybody there. As they were kissing, the skies opened up and it poured rain. Everyone scattered for their cars but he had a different idea and dragged his wife to the cabin.

"Eric! What are you doing? We should get to the limo."

"Not yet. I need to touch you, hold you, and your pirate doesn't want to share with everyone else just yet."

"Eric..."

He spun her around and walked his fingers down the tattoo along her spine. She had surprised him with it a few months ago and had the final work done just a couple of weeks ago. He still couldn't pronounce the words but it was Scottish Gaelic saying she belonged to the pirate, surrounded with Celtic knots so that the letters and the designs mixed; on either side of that design across her shoulder blades were outstretched angel wings.

"What does this say?"

"Eric..."

"Mimi."

She half smirked, half smiled.

"I belong to the pirate."

"Yes, you do and the pirate needs to make sure you are okay." He held her close, wrapping himself around her back. His hands spread over her abdomen. "And how is Surprise?"

"Surprise is smaller than a golf ball right now. He or she is fine."

"You sure? Maybe I should check?"

"Eric! People are waiting for us. You have the whole carnival planned for the reception. The foundation kids are all looking forward to it."

"You do realize that wet, your dress is almost transparent?"

Her eyes got wide and she ran to the mirror.

"I can't go out there like this!" Her hair had come undone, too. Between the transparent fabric, the leather harness, and the tumbled hair, he was never going to make it through the reception.

"I believe that is what I was saying. It will dry faster if you take it off. Want some help?"

Epilogue

Forty-five minutes later, the rain had stopped and the damn pirate had an ear-to-ear grin on his face.

"You are horrible."

"And you just pledged to love me forever despite it, in front of everyone we know."

"My legs feel like rubber."

"If that was supposed to make me feel bad, you are way off." He spooned her against him and nibbled on the back of her neck.

"Hey! No love bites, you. That is what the tattoo was for. I'm marked now." She was giggling; at best he only partly believed her and she knew it. "It would serve you right to have a daughter. Then when she is a teenager you can worry about some guy marking her as his."

He went dead still.

"I'll kill him."

She laughed at him.

"You won't be able to do a single thing about it. But with you as her father and me as her mother, she's more likely to be marking a man as hers."

"Oh God."

"We need to get dressed and go to the carnival."

Fifteen minutes later, they peeked out of the door of the cabin to see the limo was the only car left in the field.

"Where do you think Steve and Audi are?"

"Beats me. With Audi not getting in till the middle of the night, we never got to introduce them before the ceremony." Eric crowded her against the side of the limo with that look in his eye. "Eric Tolland, you cannot be serious?"

"Come on, I never got to go to prom and now I have the prettiest girl at the party. There has to be a privacy window."

"Maybe." She turned around and opened the door. One look inside and she slammed it shut again. "Was that my sister?"

"Um, you mean the woman straddling my best man? Yeah, I think it was." Eric started banging on the window. "Hey, you two. If you're going to be a while we can go back to the cabin."

Groaning and then muffled yelling and cursing could be heard from in the car. Five minutes later, the window descended and Audi peeked her head out. Her face was now as candy apple red as her hair.

"Not a God damned word, either one of you. I mean it."

Of course they just cracked up laughing.

ABOUT THE AUTHOR

Best selling author L.C. Giroux writes smart, sexy, fun, contemporary and new adult romance novels. She has written over 12 books that are as much about the love of a family as about any one couple. Romance might be an odd fit after an architecture degree and careers in cosmetics and molecular biology but five minutes into their first date she knew she had met her future husband. Twenty years later, a kid, their fair share of richer poorer sickness and health she still believes in a happy ending.

Read excerpts of her work at www.lcgiroux.com

***

69718700R00136

Made in the USA
San Bernardino, CA
20 February 2018